YEARLING BOOKS are designed especially to entertain and enlighten young people. Patricia Reilly Giff, consultant to this series, received her bachelor's degree from Marymount College and a master's degree in history from St. John's University. She holds a Professional Diploma in Reading and a Doctorate of Humane Letters from Hofstra University. She was a teacher and reading consultant for many years, and is the author of numerous books for young readers.

ECHOHAWK

by Lynda Durrant

A YEARLING BOOK

Published by
Bantam Doubleday Dell Books for Young Readers
a division of
Bantam Doubleday Dell Publishing Group, Inc.
1540 Broadway
New York, New York 10036

Visit us on the Web! www.bdd.com

**Educators and librarians, visit the BDD Teacher's
Resource Center at www.bdd.com/teachers**

ISBN: 0-440-41438-5

Reprinted by arrangement with Houghton Mifflin Company

Printed in the United States of America

November 1998

10 9 8 7 6 5 4 3 2

OPM

CONTENTS

AUTHOR'S NOTE

Wulamocawapallanewa—He Speaks Truly of the White Hawk—is Echohawk's name in Mohican. As much as I wanted to use the authentic name, Wulamocawapallanewa just wasn't feasible.

CHAPTER ONE

Camp: August 1738

JONATHAN STARR WAS WATCHING ANTS.

He sat on his favorite hollow log, the one by the creek, watching an army of ants march across his legs and onto the log. They marched in single file in an orderly, purposeful way.

No ant tried to walk ahead of another. Groups of ants were carrying bits of leaves and debris from the forest floor over their heads and climbing the wrinkles in the coarsely woven homespun cloth of Jonathan's pants. They scrambled over his logs and down again by the hundreds, thousands, millions, or so it seemed to him.

He sighed happily. There was nothing Jonathan liked better than going into deep woods alone, because there was so much to learn in the woods—about the animals and himself. He had learned that if he waited long enough, or moved quietly enough, everything in the forest came to him.

Once he'd crept so close to a deer and her twin fawns that he could see the small cloud of gnats buzzing around their eyes and noses. It had taken him close to an hour to stalk them. Another time he had sat motionless by the creek (*his* creek was how he liked to think of it) and watched a sleepy raccoon family crawl out of the log (his log). They picked the purple huckleberries that grew along the creek bed and washed each berry with their tiny, humanlike hands before eating it.

Another time he had sat on his log making a small popping sound with his lips for an entire morning. One by one, curious rabbits had come out of their burrows under the tree roots to see what he was up to.

"Jonathan," his mother called out, "have you been playing in the woods again? Come sit by the fire—you must be cold."

Cold? It's August, Jonathan thought.

Jonathan, his father, his two brothers, and his sister had counted one hundred fifty paces on the path from the creek to the cabins. Another one hundred fifty paces behind him lay the Hudson River. His creek lay right in the middle.

Through the dense trees, he could just see his mother standing alongside their cabin. She was frowning, with her hands on her hips. She looked angry, and it wasn't even dinnertime yet.

"Jonathan Starr, I mean *now*! The Indians will get you."

"Don't scare him, Celia," he heard his father say from the woodpile. Then there was no sound in the hot, sleepy woods except for his father's axe chopping into the wood.

Jonathan hunched over so his mother couldn't see him. Sitting by the creek, he saw the roofs and chimneys of the two one-room log cabins huddled in the forest like a tiny fortress against the world. The only doors faced each other, and there were no windows.

The two men—Mr. Robert Spence and Jonathan's father, Ethan Starr—had worked hard all spring cutting down the trees for their cabins. They used axes and saws brought all the way from South Carolina.

It had taken a month from sunup to sundown to cut the trees, cut the grooves in the ends, square the sides, and stack the logs to make the walls. It took another month to find branches tall enough to fit as gables for the roof. Carefully, the men saved the bark for roof shingles.

While the men built the cabins, the women used their plows and horses, also brought from South Carolina, to plow the newly cleared forest. They tried to plow around the giant roots of the trees their husbands had cut down. It was hard, hot work. The plows would catch in the tangle of roots that grew under the forest floor like a vast underground spider's web.

Next spring, plowing would wait until the men and horses cleared away the roots. This last spring, they had had to plant the corn, squash, and beans quickly so Mr. and Mrs. Spence and the Starrs could survive the winter.

Winters were much colder in the colony of New York than in the colony of South Carolina. Jonathan had heard his father and Mr. Spence describing snow that covered entire cabins with just the chimneys sticking out, like a pipe sticking out of an old man's beard. The growing season was shorter, too. Unless there was enough food to last six months, they didn't have a chance.

The Spences and the Starrs were grateful for the corn that grew so quickly. Jonathan thought of corn bread, johnnycakes, corn flapjacks next March, when the maple syrup would be ready, and corn pudding made with molasses. With the deer and wild turkey in the forest for meat, they could survive.

Their pumpkin patch was doing well, too. The thought of pumpkin pies and pumpkin puddings for Christmas dinner made his mouth water. Maybe it was close to dinnertime.

Jonathan grew tired of watching ants. Today he would try to catch fish with his hands. He and his father had once watched a bear fish that way along the riverbank. There were so many fish in his creek, surely he could wait until one swam into his hand the way they would swim into a bear's paw—if the bear was patient enough.

"Jonathan! I said now!"

He crouched down motionless next to the creek. The rock pool in front of him was as clean as the air, and as stuffed with fish as a barrel full of pickles. Slowly, he lowered his right hand into the water. A few fish swam away in alarm but then resumed their course. One fish was almost in his hand trap. Another inch or so . . .

A noise. A whisper? Jonathan kept his body still but raised his head up slowly in the direction of the noise. Something there smelled like smoke and not like an animal.

Not an animal.

Hoo, hoo, hoo, hoo.

Owl calls sounded from one end of the forest to the other. *Those aren't owls,* he thought. *Not in daylight.* He caught his breath in his throat. All other birdsong had stopped as though even the birds were holding their breath.

Steps, a lot of them, but slower and quieter than a bear's steps. Bears didn't travel in groups of . . . how many steps? How many walkers? A lot . . . more than a bear with cubs.

Jonathan's heart started pounding, his blood roared in waves in his ears. Cold sweat poured out of his hands and dripped down his forehead.

The smoke smell was even stronger.

Not like an animal.

In one swift movement he left the creek bed and crawled feet first into the hollow log. The raccoon family had already left their home for the day. He'd watched them eating fish just that morning, holding and eating each fish as if it were corn on the cob. They were hiding someplace, someplace safe.

As the steps grew closer, he could smell more smoke—smoke and the sharp smell of clean water.

Jonathan kept still and used his keen eyesight and

hearing. He could see the smoke now; it was much too late in the afternoon for fog. It *was* smoke. Smoke and bright bits of red flowers? No, it was fire—fire, smoke, and the scent of clean water.

The only sound in the hot sleepy woods was his father's axe, splitting wood for the fireplace.

Then the forest around Jonathan exploded into noise. He heard sharp yips and high-pitched yelps that sounded exactly like a fox when he is inches from catching a rabbit—a joyous hunting sound. Fire arrows streaked through the air; the smoke of gunpowder filled the forest.

"Jonathan! Jonathan!" he heard his father shout. "Stay where you are!"

The cabins were on fire. Jonathan saw sheets of flame rising higher and higher in the summer sky. He could hear screams and musket shots. Then the screaming stopped.

The forest was silent except for the rushing sound of hot wind and smoke through the pines and Jonathan's ragged gasps for breath. His stomach lurched. He put his hands over his mouth, but his midday meal came up anyway, splashing over his hands and the inside of the log, flowing into the brown creek mud.

Corn pudding. The pale-yellow river hit the creek water and spread out like a fan. The fan grew bigger and touched the other side of the creek bed. The sour smell stung the air.

They're going to find me.

His skin was cold, as cold as December, and he could

not stop trembling. The forest filled with noises again. He could hear Blaze and Brownie whinnying in fear and then soft sounds—voices?—quieting the horses.

If I can hear them, they can hear me.

The whole log sounded with Jonathan's pounding heart and sobbing, gasping breaths.

My own noise is my enemy.

The kittens, he thought, in the barn back in South Carolina: they could be absolutely silent when they didn't want to be found, as motionless and silent as stones.

I'm a kitten hiding in the hayloft. No one will find me if I'm a kitten in a hayloft.

He heard steps again, but faster, and the tread was heavier this time. The walkers were not as cautious now. They were running. He heard the horses trotting behind the steps.

Splashing. His creek—they were across from his log.

Jonathan burrowed deeper into the raccoons' home. He saw a swish of calico go by, dragging on the ground. His father's axe and Mr. Spence's saw flashed in the sunlight. He saw more calico cloth and the sleeve of a dark wool jacket. He smelled the sweet smell of the horses and saw Brownie's hooves splashing through the brown mud and yellow corn pudding.

Then many voices rising in questions and falling in anger. One of them was shouting.

Go away. Stop arguing and go away.

A ring of moccasined feet surrounded the front of the log.

I'm a silent kitten stone.

A tattooed arm reached into the log; the hand curled around his wrist like a snare and pulled him out. A sturdy red-brown man with black eyes and black braids to his waist looked back at him in surprise. The man smiled and hid him under Mr. Spence's wool cloak. The man's skin smelled like clean water.

Wrapped in hot, woolen darkness, frozen in terror like a rabbit cornered by wolves, Jonathan clung to the man's body and hid. There were hours—maybe days—of clinging and darkness.

Voices again—three this time. One was the shouting voice he'd heard back at the log, another the dry, reedy voice of an old man. And the third was the voice of the man holding him, the man who smelled like clean water.

The wool cloak parted and the man who smelled like clean water held him up. Jonathan was as still as a stone as he looked right into the old man's face.

The old man was ancient. Long white hair hung to his waist, and his skin was as red and wrinkled as a dried apple.

Everyone started talking at once. Jonathan glanced around him quickly. There were twenty people, maybe more, standing in front of the Hudson River. They surrounded him; there was no place to run or hide.

The man who smelled like clean water shouted to be heard above the others.

The old man spoke, and the other voices fell away.

He must be their king, Jonathan thought to himself. *Their . . . their sachem. He's a sachem.*

Just remembering one of their words made him feel better.

The man who smelled like clean water set him on the ground. But Jonathan's legs were as weak as creek water, and he slumped to his knees.

The angry man was shouting again. Jonathan curled into a tight ball. His mind was blank, like his older brother's school slate wiped clean of charcoal after a hard day's lessons.

The angry man kicked dirt in Jonathan's hair and face again and again.

The sachem held up his right hand and spoke for a long time. As the sachem spoke, the angry man kicked more dirt. Jonathan shut his eyes as the fine dust covered his face like gunpowder. The grit stung his cheeks like tiny bullets.

The sachem stopped speaking. Jonathan opened his eyes. The man who smelled like clean water held out his hand, and Jonathan took it. As they walked away, Jonathan looked back at the group by the river. Standing near the man who'd kicked dirt in his face was a boy about his age. They both glared at him with more hatred than he'd seen in his whole life.

He held on tighter to the man's hand, the man who smelled like clean water. Questions tumbled around inside him: Where was he? How would his family find him? Why was he by himself? What did these people want with him?

They walked to a low-standing building shaped like a turtle shell. It was covered in birch bark and animal skins and lashed together with long, thin branches of hickory. Smoke was coming out of a small hole in the top.

Above the doorframe was a piece of wood. Carved into it was a turtle that looked like a six-pointed star. The head and tail, the four arms and legs, made up the points; the shell was a series of squares radiating out from the center.

The man who smelled like clean water took off Jonathan's shoes, pants, and shirt and tossed them into a little pile next to the wigwam. His shoes seemed to stare back at him, the tongues hanging out in surprise. The man inspected Jonathan's hands and elbows. He looked behind Jonathan's ears.

"You are so dirty," the man said. "No one washes you? I could grow potatoes behind those ears."

English! Jonathan stared at him in shock. The man had six-pointed turtles tattooed on his chest. There were wampum strings braided into his hair. His muscles were like smooth iron. How could a man who looked like this speak English? Jonathan looked into the man's eyes, ready to ask his questions, but held back. The man's stern black eyes seemed bottomless; they pulled him in.

"They only wash me when they can catch me," he told the man. "But you can grow potatoes back there if you want to."

The man blinked. He nodded gravely, but a smile played on his lips.

"What's your name, sir?"

"Glickihigan." The man put his musket down within easy reach. "In English that means 'Gunsight.'"

It was dark inside the wigwam except for a fire, five logs arranged as a star burning at its center. Through the dim, smoky air, Jonathan could just make out a figure sitting next to the fire. Only the center of the figure's face glowed orange in the firelight. The rest of the face was covered in black ashes.

Jonathan looked closely at the face. The glowing nose and cheeks were streaked in tears, the ashes washed away.

The man pointed to the figure. "My last words in English to you are these. We are Mohicans. Our sachem is my wife's brother. Our son has died, and our sachem said we can keep you in his place. You are here to make her laugh again. This is your mother."

Two boys hid behind a log in a hollow on the riverbank.

"Echohawk," the younger boy said, "do you know why a woodchuck has no hair on its belly?"

Echohawk smiled. He always liked his brother's stories.

Echohawk, twelve-year-old son of Glickihigan and older brother to seven-year-old Bamaineo, could not remember a time when his name was Jonathan. The memory of the cabins was gone, like the fire that had destroyed them eight years ago.

His earliest memory was of lying flat in the medicine hut so every drop of his white blood could be replaced with Mohican blood. He had been proud, even then, of not crying (well, maybe a few whimpers when the sachem nicked his throat with a long flint knife). His blood ceremony must have been been a long time ago, because he hadn't understood most of what was said. Also, his mother had made him new moccasins for the occasion.

Now those same moccasins fit into the palm of his hand.

He had come into his name because his yellow-brown eyes were the same color as a hawk's, and his eyesight was just as keen and his gaze just as piercing. But it was more than that. The hawk was his spirit-brother. His parents had recognized the fierce, solitary spirit, or echo, of the hawk inside their older son.

He could hunt like a hawk as well. He could stay motionless in a tree waiting for small game—rabbits, raccoons, and woodchucks—to come out of their burrows to sun themselves in the clearings and eat the pasture grass. He could shoot with his bow and arrows what others couldn't even see.

"Mother, I have returned," he would say as he entered the turtle wigwam and laid the rabbits, raccoons, woodchucks, and wild turkeys at her feet. She would smile and pull his ears playfully.

These small animals were used for food. But it was the fur the family really wanted. The boys' mother used the skins to make warm moccasins, robes, and caps for the long, bitter winters. She soaked the skins in water and hung them over a smoking fire to tan them. After that, the skins were attached to a stout pole, and she would pull and pull them to make them soft.

A tiny, sharp bone was used to poke holes in the hides. They were sewn together with bone needles and thin strips of leather.

"Echohawk, why does a woodchuck have no hair on its belly?"

"Why, little brother?"

"Windigo, the Evil One, wanted—"

"Wait."

The boys crouched lower behind the log as soft mud curled around their toes. They practiced their hunt breathing—pulling the air into themselves with their stomachs and not their chests—so as to make no sound.

They were so low to the ground, their long braids swept into the soft river mud. Their forearms rested on the log for balance. Echohawk's arms were the same tan color as his buckskin shirt. Bamaineo's arms were the soft, glowing color of freshly cut cedar.

Echohawk's eyes focused on the opposite bank. His ears had picked up the sound they'd been waiting for.

A mountain lion and her two cubs padded softly down the west bank of the river. The lioness was the silver-gray of old weatherbeaten logs. Her cubs were tawny-brown and speckled like fawns.

She hid the cubs behind a fallen log. Echohawk saw two pairs of cub ears above the log, like four baby turtles sunning themselves in a row.

The mother drank warily, keeping her eyes up and watchful. She drank from the river for a long time. When she'd had enough, she made a low sound in her throat. Only then did the cubs clamber over the log and bound toward the river. As the cubs played, their mother kept a sharp eye out for predators. When she was thirsty again, she pushed the cubs behind the log once more.

But the cubs didn't want to hide. They tumbled over each other, splashing in the water. They practiced hunting by pouncing on each other.

They had been here yesterday too. When the sun was still half in his night blanket, the lion family had come down to this very spot to drink.

"I told you I saw them, Bamy," Echohawk murmured. "We can come down here every morning this spring and summer to see them."

The lioness looked up and narrowed her eyes. With one short snarl from their mother, the cubs stopped playing and followed her up the steep west bank of the river. They were soon gone in the thick underbrush.

"Will they come back?" Bamaineo asked. "My name is Bamaineo. Bamy is a baby name."

"Everyone calls you Bamy. Talking!" Echohawk shouted crossly. "How could I break the first rule of hunting? I wanted you to see them, little brother."

"I know why."

Their mother had died the previous moon, and the brothers looked everywhere for signs that she was still with them: the lion cubs and the lioness; the twin stars near the moon; the way two clouds always followed a larger one in the sky; the way two creeks always joined to make a river.

Their faces were painted in black ashes to show the world their sorrow.

"We were not really hunting, Echohawk, just looking, so it does not really count."

Echohawk was so angry, he rolled the log they were hiding behind into the river. It landed with a loud splash. "If they do not come back here, I will find them. I promise, Bamy," he said through clenched teeth. "We will see them again."

"Windigo, the Evil One, wanted to catch every animal in the forest so he would not have to hunt anymore," Bamaineo continued. "He asked the Woodchuck Sachem for a magic bag. The Woodchuck Sachem pulled every hair out of his belly to make the magic bag. Windigo took every animal—all the elk, the deer, the moose, the foxes, the bears, the lions, the rabbits, the raccoons, even the mice—and put them all in the bag.

"But the Woodchuck Sachem was very angry and set all the animals free again. 'The animals all would have died in the bag,' he said, 'and the People would have become weak with hunger. Only when animals are hunted are they strong. Only when the People hunt are they strong.'"

Echohawk stared at the spot where the lioness had heard him talking.

"Are you still angry, Echohawk?" Bamaineo asked warily. "Look at your log."

As they watched, the log Echohawk had pushed into the river floated to midstream. It picked up speed, then spun around the bend and out of sight. Echohawk knew it floated south, toward the village of *Saratoga-on-the-Hudson.*

16

"Do you ever wonder, Bamy, what the English camp looks like? What the English look like?"

Bamaineo shrugged his shoulders. "Sometimes."

Echohawk took a deep breath and let it out slowly. "No. I am no longer angry. We should go home."

CHAPTER THREE *The Fish Running Moon*

ECHOHAWK AND BAMAINEO WENT HOME just as the sun was full in the sky. They stayed on the east side of the river and walked upstream. When the mosquitoes bit their necks, Echohawk remembered, too late, that they had forgotten to rub their exposed skin with bear grease mixed with cedar oil to keep the mosquitoes away.

"Run!" he shouted, hoping to outrun the mosquitoes. The brothers were hot and sweating by the time they reached the camp.

Four wigwams made up the camp. To Echohawk, they had always looked like giant turtles that had crawled out of the river to sun themselves on the beach. The wigwams were far enough apart for privacy, close enough together for protection.

The first wigwam was Makwa, or the Bear clan. The clan leader, Makwa, lived there with his wife, Makwasi; his son, Gahko; and his three little daughters. The second wigwam was Nehjao, or the Wolf clan. Nehjao lived there with his oldest son, Tooksetuk—which meant Little Wolf—his wife, and two younger sons.

On higher ground and closer to the trees was the royal Tanebao, or Great Turtle, clan of Tanebao Sachem. Tanebao Sachem lived there with his two wives and all their children. Echohawk and Bamaineo's own home, the second Turtle clan wigwam, lay close by.

A wide fire ditch ran through the center of the camp. The fires were used to smoke fish and venison for the winter. North of the wigwams was the food storehouse, built of sturdy logs to keep the bears and wolves away. A fire pit for making maple sugar was dug in front of the storehouse. North of the storehouse lay the corn rows and vegetable patches. North of the garden lay the playground and target range.

"Echohawk, listen."

They heard laughing and splashing coming from upriver near the waterfall.

"Everyone is swimming but us," Bamaineo said bitterly. "I hate mourning. I hate it." He kicked the ground in front of him.

"You hate it for the wrong reason," Echohawk said quietly.

Their mother had always laid fresh, sweet pine needles in a thick layer on the floor, so the wigwam smelled like fresh pine and woodsmoke. She made fresh mats out of the rush grasses that grew along the river every spring. These mats were fastened to the inside walls and were used to keep out the rain and block the cold wind in winter. They also used the mats she made for the sleeping platforms, built knee high off the ground to keep them warm and dry in all weathers.

Now the turtle wigwam was in disarray. Last night's rain had leaked through the roof and made the pine needles soggy. The animal skins used for bedding were wet and becoming stiff. The rush mats stank like a swamp.

Bamaineo opened the door flap and crept inside.

"The starfire is out! Echohawk!" he shouted.

Echohawk threw open the door flap and hurried inside. The starfire *was* out. He lay on his stomach to get a closer look.

In the darkness, Echohawk saw one tiny red glow near the center of the starfire. The five logs that made up the starfire were as cold as stone.

Nothing, *nothing* was more important than keeping the starfire burning. Hadn't the starfires been burning since the beginning, when the Creator, Kishelemukong, allowed stars to fall from the sky to ignite the flames? Sometimes during blizzards or heavy rain, their mother had stayed up all night to stoke the starfire. The boys had been told again and again that if the starfire goes out, the wigwam dies. And if the wigwam dies, the people die with it.

There was no time to lose.

"Bamy, use pine needles, your hair, anything, to keep that ember going! I will find twigs and kindling."

But Bamaineo was already touching the end of one long braid to the tiny glow. One by one, he lit pine needles from his burning hair and gently blew on them to keep them burning.

Echohawk raced into the woods and began picking up twigs, bark, last autumn's leaves, rotten wood, anything that might burn. When he returned, Bamaineo set the twigs in a small arch over the burning pine needles in the center of the starfire. He gently placed the leaves and bark over the burning needles.

He blew on the arch softly, watching to see if the glow burned brighter. But nothing happened. "The twigs and leaves are too wet from last night's rain, Echohawk."

Echohawk grabbed handfuls of brown pine needles from under his sleeping platform and placed them under the twigs in the center of the starfire. A tiny flame shot out of the center and leaped upward. They added larger twigs and kindling and watched anxiously as the wet wood sputtered and steamed. They put on more handfuls of dried pine needles. As the flame grew hotter, the twigs stopped steaming and soon were burning; finally the logs caught fire. The starfire came slowly back to life. The boys breathed easier; no one was going to die today.

"What a good thing our father is not here," Bamaineo said anxiously. "What a good thing the men are deer hunting."

Echohawk nodded. Glickihigan would never know that the Turtle clan's starfire had almost died.

When they were satisfied that the starfire was burning

well, Echohawk went back into the woods for more kindling. His arms were full when he returned to the camp.

Makwa's son, Gahko, blocked his way on the path. Gahko and Echohawk were equal in size and weight.

"A warrior carrying wood? That is the work of a woman," Gahko said scornfully. He stepped closer.

Echohawk glanced quickly at the turtle wigwam. Smoke was coming out of the ceiling flap. Bamaineo had kept the starfire burning while he was gone.

As Echohawk looked away, Gahko pushed his shoulder hard.

Echohawk fixed on Gahko his fierce, piercing hawk gaze. He could see a flicker of fear in Gahko's eyes. He narrowed his own eyes into slits.

"Now I remember why you are here," Gahko shouted. There was a trace of shakiness in his voice. "My father says you are supposed to do the work of women. White eyes."

Echohawk scanned Gahko's body for weapons. Gahko's long black hair still dripped river water from his morning swim. No weapons. He threw the kindling in Gahko's face.

As Gahko stepped back, Echohawk kicked his legs out from under him, and Gahko fell to the forest floor. Echohawk was on him in an eye blink and they wrestled and scratched, trying to pin each other on the ground, hitting anywhere they could. Echohawk saw Gahko pick up a short, thick branch with his left hand. As Gahko tried to swing his weapon, Echohawk caught his wrist and squeezed hard. Gahko's grip loosened and the branch fell to the ground.

"Stop it, right now," Gahko's mother shouted. Makwasi pulled the boys apart, then lifted them to their feet. "Gahko, go back to the wigwam. Repair the fishing nets before your father gets home. Now!"

Gahko shook his mother's hand off his arm. His shoulder pushed against Echohawk's shoulder as he passed. "White eyes," he muttered in his ear.

Without saying a word, Makwasi picked up all the scattered kindling Echohawk had brought from the woods. She marched into the turtle wigwam with him trotting at her heels.

Bamaineo was so startled he sprang to his feet. No woman but his mother had ever been inside his home.

"Your logs are too small." Makwasi dropped the kindling in the fur end of the wigwam. "Your logs should be big enough to sit on. As their center ends burn, push the logs forward and replace them with new logs. You never watched her take care of the starfire?"

Silence.

She put her hands on her hips. "Too busy daydreaming of hunting, as though that is the only thing that matters. I used to gather wood with her. I will leave wood by your front door flap in the mornings." She gave Echohawk a hard look. "The Bear clan has never liked you; I will leave the wood in her memory."

"Thank you, Makwasi," Bamaineo said softly.

Makwasi marched out of the wigwam just as quickly

as she had come in. The door flap closed behind her, leaving the boys in semidarkness.

"Women are weak, but mothers are strong," Echohawk said as he wiped the blood from his mouth. His hand came away streaked with blood and black mourning paint.

"You should wash your mouth before our father returns."

The brothers smiled at each other, their teeth and eyes stark white against the black paint.

"Gahko looks worse," Echohawk said.

For the summer the men and boys had built roofed porches on the south sides of the wigwams. Echohawk and Bamaineo spent the long summer days (when they weren't swimming or hunting) eating fresh berries, roasted corn, fresh game, and fish on their porch. They brought the sleeping mats outside and slept on the porch at night. When the brothers woke in the dawntime, they saw mist curling skyward on the river, and arrows of waterfowl skimming the water on their way to the marshes.

Late that afternoon Glickihigan and the rest of the men came home from hunting. The brothers were waiting for him.

"Glickihigan!"

"Glickihigan!"

"Bad hunting this time," Glickihigan said as he laid his musket on the summer-porch floor.

Their father looked tired. The mourning paint black ashes mixed with walnut oil—had settled into streaks in the wrinkles around his eyes and mouth. He sat hunched over, leaning his head against the middle porch pole.

"How many deer did you get?" Bamaineo asked.

Echohawk watched as Makwa sat down empty-handed on his summer porch. The entire Bear clan turned as one to glare at him. Echohawk heard Makwa shout, "Bad luck." Nehjao sat down empty-handed, too.

"How many deer did you get?" Bamaineo asked again, louder this time. "Father? How many—"

Echohawk pressed his forehead on the back of his brother's neck. "None," he whispered softly.

"The Fish Running Moon is coming in two suns," Glickihigan said. "Tomorrow we will repair our nets."

"I killed three rabbits this afternoon," Echohawk said. "Two of them were running away from my arrows when I shot them. Father, you know I never miss. I should have gone on the deer hunt."

"I know you never miss. But we saw no deer. None. What will we eat this winter? And someone must watch Bamaineo now."

Echohawk sighed. "The rabbits are roasted, Father. Our evening corn is ready."

"I picked some huckleberries," Bamaineo added.

"It is good to be home."

Their large nets were made of grapevines tightly woven together. The cross points were tied with grapevine bark to tighten the weave. The tough inner fiber of the vine was used for the rope at the top. These large nets could be tossed into the river, then pulled closed like a drawstring bag.

All the next day, the men and boys inspected the nets for weak spots and places where the bark had come untied. The women and girls cleared debris out of the fire ditch.

That evening everyone looked up at the Fish Running Moon and thought about the previous year's catch. There had been so many fish. They had dried enough to last them through the entire winter.

In the dawntime the three clans took their nets to the river. The men and boys climbed the rocks next to the waterfall, found their favorite places along the upper riverbank, and peered into the smooth water. The calm, deep pool above the falls was as clear as the air; they could see all the way to the bottom. The herring, salmon, and trout were gill to gill, tail to tail, they were so crowded together.

The Turtle clan was first. Glickihigan, Echohawk, and Bamaineo tossed their net into the water and slowly pulled the rope together at the top. They tugged and struggled to bring the net ashore. It bulged with fish. As the water poured out of the net and onto the riverbank, the net shuddered and twisted like a trapped animal.

Next, the Wolf clan tossed their net into the river. Nehjao, Tooksetuk, and the other two boys drew the rope together at the top and pulled in their net. Another good catch! Echohawk was already thinking about fresh fish for evening corn; they could feast all night if they wanted to.

Finally, the Bear clan tossed in their net. Makwa and Gahko drew the rope together slowly at the top and pulled in the net. It too was crowded with fish. The fishermen smiled at one another. There would be enough fish for the longest winter.

As the Bear clan pulled their net toward shore, the weave tore and the fish poured back into the pool.

They all watched in horror as the fish swam away and over the waterfall.

"White eyes," Gahko shouted, "my father is right! You bring us bad luck! You made our net break!"

"You didn't check your net," Echohawk shouted back. "I saw you skip over the cross points. It was your fault!"

"This white boy brings bad luck to the People," Makwa said in a low, cold voice. "He should go back home."

Echohawk scowled at the identical, sneering faces of Makwa and Gahko. "It was not my fault!" he shouted. He threw himself at Gahko in pure, hot rage.

Glickihigan wrapped his arms around his son from behind. His arms were as strong as a bear's.

"You will stop. You will stop," Glickihigan whispered in his ear. "Stop."

"This white boy should go home," Makwa repeated. "Bad luck."

Echohawk ducked his head toward the Turtle clan's net. It had stopped moving and the fish were losing that bright silver look they had had when first caught.

Bad luck.

The bad net, the bad deer hunt, the starfire almost out, losing the lioness and her cubs. Am I bad luck? he wondered.

Glickihigan, behind him, rested his hands on Echohawk's shoulders. "The Fish Running Moon always gives us enough fish for the winter, Makwa. We will take our net back to camp. I will come back here and lend it to you."

When they returned home, the women had already built the smoking fires. The Turtle clan cleaned their catch and hung their own fish over the fire. The fish belonged to everyone in the camp. The Bear clan's lost fish meant less fish for everyone.

Bamaineo took some of the fish entrails into the forest so the animals could enjoy the Fish Running Moon, too. The rest would be used as fertilizer in the vegetable garden.

The Bear clan came back at sundown with a small catch.

On the summer porches that evening they all ate fresh fish, tiny roasted new corn, and wild strawberries. When night fell, the People sat in the soft air of late spring to watch the stars come out and the Fish Running Moon drop out of the sky for another year.

"Father, the Bear clan could go back to the river tomorrow with a net," Bamaineo said.

"Our sister the river is very generous with her fish," Glickihigan replied. "But if we go back tomorrow, and the next day and the next, soon she will have no fish to give us."

"But it would only be the one time—"

"No, Bamaineo. The four elements—the earth, the plants, the animals, and the People—all hang in careful balance with one another. Take away too much of one, and everything falls."

"Am I bad luck?" Echohawk asked quickly.

Glickihigan scowled. "Makwa's son is lazy and makes bad nets. Laziness is not bad luck."

"The starfire almost went out, two suns ago. While you were deer hunting. Bad luck."

Bamaineo cut in: "Echohawk went to look for kindling, but everything was so wet and he was gone for such a long time. He told me to use anything that would burn."

"I see."

Their father was silent. The brothers could sense him sitting motionless in the darkness.

"I was wondering why one of Bamaineo's braids is so much shorter than the other. We will all have to take turns watching the starfire now. Forgetting is not bad luck. But, Bamaineo, do not use your hair for kindling again."

Bamaineo laughed.

Glickihigan knew what Echohawk was thinking. "Your mother was sick a long time, my son. She was not well before you came to her wigwam. Windsong had an echo in her heart."

The brothers gasped. No one ever said the names of the dead out loud unless it was for a very, very good reason.

"The person, the spirit; the animal, its spirit; they are all one because time travels in a circle," their father explained. "When you meet your mother again, she will tell you this herself. Bad luck did not kill her."

Bamaineo said, "It makes no sense. But if I understand tomorrow, will I see her tomorrow?"

"Echohawk," their father said softly, "when you show your anger, your enemy has already won."

"I had every right to be angry," Echohawk retorted. "Gahko was blaming his laziness on me."

"That is not what I said," Glickihigan replied, softer still. "You will think about what I have said to you."

"Father, answer my question. Will I see her—"

"Bamaineo," Glickihigan said patiently, "you too will think about what I have said to you. Now go to sleep."

CHAPTER FOUR

"IT IS HOT ALREADY. When can we swim in the *Hudson* again?" Bamaineo complained. They were washing bowls in the river before morning corn. It was seven suns into the Fish Running Moon.

"Bamaineo, what did you say?" Glickihigan shouted crossly.

The brothers looked at him surprise. Their father never spoke to them that way.

"I said—I want to swim," he stammered. "She would want us to swim. My face is sweating under this paint."

"That is not what I meant." Their father pointed to the river. "What is the name of our river, Bamaineo?"

"The Muhekunetuk," he said in a small voice.

"What does it mean, Echohawk?"

"The water is never still. Because of the tides that come up from the Gishikshawkipet, the Sun's Salt Sea," he explained.

"The earth is the moon's mother and he misses her,"

Bamaineo said softly. "But when he tries to draw her to him, only the water moves."

"The Muhekunetuk is our river," Echohawk said. "The Mohican River."

Glickihigan stood up. "Don't you ever call the Muhekunetuk the *Hudson* again, do you hear me?"

"So can we swim in the Muhekunetuk?"

"Ask me about swimming and games in six suns," Glickihigan replied. "You are in mourning."

Bamaineo threw his bowl in the mud. "But I'm hot now!"

"Go to the wigwam, Bamaineo, now!"

Bamaineo stomped off to the Turtle wigwam. "I know she would not mind," he shouted back over his shoulder. "She would want us to swim."

"I'm hot, too," Echohawk said, "and my face itches under the paint. My brother is right. She would not mind if we swam."

"You and your brother are right, Echohawk. She would not mind. *I* mind. If you are hot, sit on the summer porch."

Echohawk picked up a large rock and dropped it into the water. *Kaplunk!* The cool water felt good on his arms and legs. "We want to swim," he said through clenched teeth.

Glickihigan sighed. "We are all so angry because she has left us here. The sorrow we can accept; the anger we cannot.

"Echohawk, Tanebao Sachem wants to talk to all of

us this morning about another deer hunt. We will hunt the Abenaki way. The Abenaki live so far to the north, they always have fewer deer in their country than we do. This time we all can go, even Bamaineo and the younger boys."

A deer hunt! Echohawk forgot about the heat and his itchy face. The boys had spent most of their lives getting ready for deer hunts: practicing tracking deer from the river, shooting with bows and arrows on the target range, walking in woods without making a sound.

"This council will be in the royal wigwam?" Echohawk asked breathlessly. "I have never been inside it."

"Yes." Glickihigan looked at him proudly. "You have been invited inside."

"Bamaineo?"

"Only if he asks me."

At midmorning, Echohawk rushed home to tell Bamaineo about the deer-hunt council.

His brother was sitting hunched over on his sleeping platform and kicking the ground beneath him. Every time he kicked, a cloud of dirt and pine needles rose up and filtered through the smoky air. It settled on the deerskin sleeping blankets, the cooking and eating bowls, the spoons, the extra moccasins and deerskin shirts, and the bearskin winter blankets.

"You missed the council, Bamy," Echohawk shouted. He knelt on the ground next to his brother. "We met in the royal wigwam. It was beautiful. The inside skins were painted with scenes from the Muhekunetuk. There were turtles on rocks and turtles in the river. And the wolf was high on the riverbank watching everyone, protecting everyone."

Bamaineo kicked the ground again.

"Stop kicking dirt everywhere. Did you ask our father when you could leave the wigwam?"

Kick.

"You have to ask him when you can leave. He won't tell you."

Kick.

"Bamaineo, we talked about a deer hunt. We can all go on this deer hunt." Echohawk peered into his brother's face and saw a flicker of interest in his eyes.

"We are in mourning, remember?" Bamaineo answered crossly. "That means no swimming, no stickball, no races."

"It is only for six more suns—you heard our father say so. And tomorrow it will be only five more suns."

Kick.

"We will hunt the Abenaki way," Echohawk said excitedly. "Their country always has fewer deer than ours. We are going to build a tall, strong fence shaped like an arrowhead with the point missing. Like this, look." Echohawk held his hands up, his elbows down and his fingers not quite touching.

"As the chasers run after the deer, the deer will run through the point and the hunters on the other side of the fence will shoot them. Little brother, Tanebao Sachem said I could be one of the hunters! He said he has been watching me. Our sachem has been watching me."

"Our father was proud," Bamaineo said crossly.

"Yes."

"And Gahko was angry."

"Our sachem said Gahko will be one of the chasers." Echohawk's face broke into a wide grin, and even his brother smiled a little.

Then Bamaineo scowled. "This hunt is not for us. All we can do is sit with itchy black paint on our faces."

Kick.

"It will take all summer to build this fence. I will need an extra in case I miss," Echohawk explained. "If you practice and become a perfect shot, I will ask you to be my extra."

"Not our father?" Bamaineo asked in astonishment.

"Glickihigan knows the way of deer so well, he will be leading the chasers.

"One more thing, little brother," Echohawk whispered. "We need more hunters, so Nehjao will cross the river into Iroquois country and ask the Mohawks to join us. He was once their captive and remembers the language."

"Mohawks!" Bamaineo exclaimed.

"They are our enemies, but if our deer are scarce, perhaps their deer are scarce, too. Tanebao Sachem says if Nehjao comes back with fifteen Mohawks, our hunt will be successful."

"But—"

"Our father is coming in," Echohawk whispered as Glickihigan stepped inside. "Ask him if you can leave the wigwam. We could practice with our bows and arrows now."

"Nothing for six suns, remember?" Bamaineo kicked the ground again. A dirt cloud rose up and settled on the starfire.

"Hunting is not playing, Bamy," Echohawk said, "not like swimming or stickball. Ask him. . . . Ask him."

"Bamaineo," Glickhigan said in a mild voice, "do you have something to ask me?"

Kick.

A cloud of dirt and pine needles landed on Echohawk's face and stuck to the black mourning paint.

"You are stubborn, Bamy," Echohawk shouted as he stood up. He spit dirt out of his mouth and yanked his brother's braids. "And you have kicked dirt everywhere. If you are not a perfect shot by the Moon of Ripe Berries, you will not be my extra!" Echohawk picked up his bow and arrows and flung open the door flap. "Be a chaser then."

"Stop calling me Bamy!" his brother shouted. "My name is Bamaineo, the Bounding Elk!"

"Stubborn Worm is a better name."

Bamaineo sprang from his sleeping platform and hit Echohawk's back as hard as he could.

Echohawk seized Bamaineo's arm and twisted it. "Dead Worm—"

"Stop! Sit on your sleeping platforms, both of you,"

their father said sternly. "Bamaineo, you will apologize to me and your brother. Then you will take everything outside. You will shake out everything you have kicked this dirt into."

Kick.

A cloud of dirt and pine needles landed on Glickihigan's feet. Silence hung in the wigwam like an evil spirit.

"I have other uses for my bow besides hunting," his father said softly. "I know why there is so much anger in you. I do not want to use my bow on you, but I will. Come, I will help you shake out the bearskins. They are much too heavy for you."

"Then can I leave?" Bamaineo spit out his words.

"What else must you do?"

Bamaineo's eyes filled with tears. "Now I know how Echohawk feels, angry all the time."

"I know he is sorry," Echohawk said softly. "I'm sorry too."

Glickihigan knelt in front of his younger son. "Shaking out the bearskins will help," he said gently. "Come."

The Turtle, Wolf, and Bear clans worked on the hunt fence all through the Fish Running Moon, the Strawberry Moon, and the Moon of the Longest Days.

They built it high above the camp, where the riverbank leveled off to grass-filled glades.

The women and girls cut long strips of deerskin out of old winter robes and sleeping blankets.

Each log was the size of a man's leg. The men and boys pounded the logs into the ground, then wove the long strips of deerskin between them to hold them upright. After it rained, the deerskin strips tightened as they dried; the logs were so close together, no one could see to the other side of the fence.

Finally, the hunt fence was ready by the Moon of Ripe Berries, the hottest time of the year.

On the night before the deer hunt, the Moon of Ripe Berries rose in the night sky. The river water glittered in the moonlight. Fifteen Mohawks and Nehjao paddled across the Muhekunetuk. Their canoes cut through the moonlit water like knives.

The next day everyone was awake before the dawntime.

In a cave near camp Makwa and Gahko banked white-hot coals around large, flat stones from the river. They covered the mouth of the cave with deerskins. When the air inside the cave became hot, the men and boys sat naked around the hot stones. Every so often someone would pour a little clean water on the stones, and steam would hiss upward.

It was hard to breathe. Echohawk pulled scalding air into his lungs at every breath. He didn't know which was worse—the hot dry air or the hot moist air.

Steam filled the dark cave, and they were all sweating hard. Soon they would not smell like smoke, tobacco, cooked food, and paints. Soon they would not smell like people and frighten the deer away. After a swim in the river, they would smell like clean water.

"How much longer do we have to stay here?" Ba maineo asked, panting. "Soon I will be too dizzy to hunt."

"You may leave now," Glickihigan said. "Swim in the Muhekunetuk. Be sure to soak your hair."

The men stayed in the cave while the boys ran whooping and hollering into the river. The cold water on his hot skin made Echohawk gasp. He swam as deep as he could, the water becoming colder and colder the farther down he went. As he swam closer to shore, he saw turtles, fish, and freshwater crabs swirling around him in the bright, sunlit water.

By the time the men were in the river, Echohawk was floating on his back. The river water pulled at his long hair. The heat from the sweathouse had made him feel sleepy. He closed his eyes. The sun had just dried his face when somebody dunked him under the water. He came up sputtering, face to face with Gahko.

"We need this fence because of you, White Eyes," Gahko said fiercely. "When are you going to leave so the deer will come back? Go home." He splashed water in Echohawk's face. "Go back across the Sun's Salt Sea where you came from."

Echohawk dove deep and swam away from him. "I will be a hunter today," he shouted when he came to the surface. "What will you be doing, chaser?"

"I can hunt as well as you," Gahko shouted back.

Back in the turtle wigwam, Glickihigan, Bamaineo, and Echohawk painted one another's arms and faces

39

with purple stripes highlighted with white. They dressed in clean moccasins, leggings, and breechcloths. They braided their hair tightly, then tied the braids back so they would stay out of the way.

Everyone else was standing around the storehouse waiting for them. Tanebao Sachem, who was also wearing the royal purple and white stripes, stood between his first wife and second wife. The second wife's children played at their feet. Makwa, Makwasi, Gahko, and the three daughters of the Bear clan stood in the middle. Nehjao, his wife, Tooksetuk, and the other two wolf sons stood on the other side of the firepit. The Mohawks stood off to the side.

When they were all quiet, their sachem raised his arms.

"Manitou, give the People a safe and successful hunt. We ask your spirit on earth, the wolf, to protect us. We are his People, the Mohicans, the Wolf People."

Tanebao Sachem looked into the face of every man and boy surrounding him. The Bear and Wolf clans all wore bright green hunt paint on their arms, chests, and faces. Even the women and girls wore dabs of green paint on their foreheads.

The Mohawks wore their usual red paint.

"Good hunting," the sachem said.

"How much longer do we have to wait, Echohawk?"

"Bamy, stop asking so many questions. You talk too much."

Echohawk, Bamaineo, Nehjao, Tooksetuk, and five

Mohawks were on their side of the deer fence waiting for the chasers.

They were sitting in tall grass teeming with insects and mice. Echohawk could hardly sit still.

It is hard to wait. My heart pounds like a drum. He took a deep breath and pressed his hands against his knees. He would never admit to being as anxious for the deer as Bamaineo.

"Echohawk." Tooksetuk sat down next to him. "This is your first deer hunt."

"Yes," Echohawk said breathlessly.

"Yes, I remember the excitement. I hope this hunt fence works, but this is not the same as hunting deer the old way. I hope you have a chance to hunt them the old way. Tracking them from the river, stalking them, knowing their ways: That is deer hunting. This is my last hunt along the Muhekunetuk."

"Why?" Bamaineo asked.

Tooksetuk ran his finger down his bowstring. "I will be leaving. I will be getting married soon," he said shyly.

"Married!" Echohawk exclaimed. "You are only two winters older than me."

"She is a Sokoki. I will be living far to the north in their country."

"What does she look like? Are you scared?" Bamaineo asked.

"Bamy! A warrior is not afraid of anything," Echohawk said.

"I have never seen her," Tooksetuk replied. "Her parents talked to my parents at the tribal meeting two summers ago. Her name is Hepte, so she must be tall and graceful like a swan. I am not scared exactly. . . ."

Hoo, hoo, hoo, hoo.

Loud owl calls sounded from one end of the glade to another.

Tooksetuk stood up. "They are here."

They took their places about one hundred paces from the fence. Echohawk heard branches breaking and leaves tearing as the animal weight tore through the forest. Something smashed against the hunt fence once, twice, but the fence held fast.

A deer burst through the opening. Nehjao took aim with his musket and fired. The deer went down.

Another deer came through. This one turned left abruptly and escaped down the riverbank.

Another deer came through. Tooksetuk and Echohawk took careful aim and let their arrows fly. Tooksetuk's arrow missed, but Echohawk's aim was true. Another deer down.

Another deer ran right down the middle. Echohawk took aim and shot it himself.

Another deer—the Mohawks shot it.

Another deer—Tooksetuk brought it down.

Another deer—Nehjao had had time to reload his musket. He fired and missed. Bamaineo brought it down.

More and more deer charged through the fence. Those the Mohicans missed the Mohawks shot. Their arrows had different feathers, so there would be no

42

question after the hunt as to who had shot what.

"To the right!" Echohawk could hear Glickihigan shouting on the other side of the fence. "To the right, turn right!"

Gahko burst through the hunt fence and ran screaming down the center of the clearing. After him charged an angry buck, brandishing his antlers like weapons. Everyone stood rooted to the ground in shock as Gahko ran past.

Too late, Echohawk thought. *Gahko is too far away now. If I shoot now, I will only hit the buck's hindquarters.*

The fight.

He remembered Gahko picking up the branch with his left hand.

His left hand. He will run farther and faster to the left than to the right.

Echohawk took aim and waited for Gahko to turn. Gahko dodged right and the buck followed, butting Gahko's shoulders with his antlers.

Turn left, Gahko. Left!

Gahko dodged left and screamed again. Echohawk shot his arrow, aiming just behind Gahko's back. The buck dodged left and lowered his head to put on another burst of speed. Echohawk's arrow sank to its feathers behind the buck's left shoulder, piercing his heart. The buck jumped straight into the air and was dead before he hit the ground.

Someone shoved Echohawk from behind and sent him flying forward into the grass.

"You tried to kill him! I saw you!" Makwa shouted.

Echohawk flipped onto his back. Makwa was standing over him, his dark eyes blazing in anger.

Jumbled confusion surrounded them. Deer were racing past and crashing to the ground. Men and boys were shooting arrows through the air and firing muskets. Mohawks and Mohicans were screaming in excitement. Bamaineo was charging toward his brother.

"He is lefthanded," Echohawk shouted as he stood up. "I knew he would dodge left. I was waiting for him to turn!"

"Makwa, stop." Nehjao stood between them. "How did you know Gahko would turn left?"

"He had already turned right once," Echohawk replied. Bamaineo threw his arms around his waist, almost knocking him down again.

Nehjao stared at Echohawk openmouthed.

"Gahko is lefthanded. I—I knew he would feel more . . . confident turning left. Just behind a deer's left shoulder is the best shot," Echohawk stammered. Makwa's musket was so close to his face, he could smell the acrid scent of gunpowder. "I was not trying to kill Gahko, I was trying to save him. I did save him, Makwa."

"I have never seen such a thing," Nehjao said. "I will tell my wife. She will write a song about you."

Another deer ran right past them, so close Echohawk could feel her hot breath on his skin. Makwa fired his musket and the deer went down beside them. As the gunsmoke cleared, Echohawk fixed his fierce hawk gaze on Makwa. He didn't care if Makwa was an elder and a clan leader.

"You know nothing about mc, Makwa," Echohawk said fiercely. "Nothing at all."

CHAPTER FIVE

SUCH A LONG SUN, Echohawk thought as he propped his back against his sleeping platform. Bamaineo was already asleep on the platform next to him.

He let himself become entranced by the starfire, which flickered, whispered, and danced in front of his heavy eyelids.

They had killed ten deer, and the Mohawks had left another five as a present. With the dried fish and vegetables, that was more than enough for even the coldest and longest winter.

It had taken a long time to carry all the deer from the clearing to the camp. In camp the deer had to be bled first so the meat wouldn't taste bitter. Now the deer hung in the storehouse; the men would take turns standing watch all night so the wolves wouldn't take the fresh meat while the rest of them slept.

That must be where Glickihigan is, Echohawk thought. *At the next Moon of Ripe Berries, I will be one of the men standing watch against the wolves.*

Echohawk heard footsteps near the door flap. "Glickihigan," he said softly, "is that you?"

"It is Wapakwe," a soft woman's voice said. "Are you still awake? Come outside."

"Wait." Echohawk scrambled to his feet. He put on his breechcloth and moccasins.

Wapakwe, Tanebao Sachem's first wife, stood waiting for him when he stepped outside. "My husband would like to talk to you before you sleep tonight," she said. She turned him toward the moonlight and lifted his face up by the chin. "Your face is dirty. Did you wash after the hunt?"

"I was too tired."

The old woman clucked like a turkey hen. "But not too tired to stay up late. She would have made you wash in the river."

"You are right, Wapakwe."

"Wash your face and arms in the Muhekunetuk," she said. "But hurry—your sachem is waiting."

"Wapakwe, what is wrong?"

Wapakwe hesitated. "He wants to talk to you."

Echohawk washed his face and arms quickly and stepped into the royal wigwam. He stood perfectly still and kept his eyes cast downward.

"Echohawk," Tanebao Sachem called to him. "Come in. I want to talk to you."

Echohawk saw Glickihigan, Makwa, and Tanebao Sachem sitting around the starfire. The air was thick with tobacco smoke. Tanebao Sachem's white hair glowed orange in the firelight.

Glickihigan and Makwa stood up. Makwa walked quickly over to Echohawk and struck his face so hard, he fell to the floor.

"Get up," Glickihigan said softly.

He stood up in a daze. The wigwam spun slowly around him.

"I did not bring you into your mother's wigwam so you could show disrespect to clan leaders. You do not talk back to Makwa. You will apologize to him now."

"I am sorry, Makwa," Echohawk whispered.

"He did not hear you."

"I am sorry, Makwa," Echohawk said, louder.

Makwa stood in front of Echohawk but would not meet his eyes.

"Makwa," Tanebao Sachem said, "we agreed you would say something to my brother-in-law's son."

"Thank you for saving my son," Makwa said stiffly.

Tanebao Sachem nodded to Makwa, and he left quickly.

"Good, that is finished. Sit here." The sachem pointed to a spot next to him.

Echohawk sat cross-legged in front of the fire and waited. The heat from the flames made the side of his face feel on fire.

"Echohawk, did you enjoy hunting today?"

"Yes, sachem," Echohawk whispered. It was so unfair! The humiliation smarted far worse than his stinging face. The starfire blurred in front of his eyes. He clenched his teeth to keep from crying.

Silence.

"Echohawk, did you enjoy hunting today?"

Glickihigan mouthed the words *Echohawk, speak up.*

"Echohawk, did you enjoy—"

"Yes, sachem," he shouted.

Tanebao Sachem jumped. "You do not have to shout."

"I am sorry," he said loudly. "Yes, very much."

"I have heard about your shooting today," Tanebao Sachem said. "Do you think you could shoot like that again?"

Echohawk's gaze wandered to the wigwam walls, to the skins painted with river turtle scenes. The flickering and wavering firelight seemed to make the turtles move. They appeared to swim and hunt right in front of him.

"Do you think you could shoot like that again?"

"Yes, sachem," he said quickly. "I think so."

"You think so." The sachem nodded. "Do you think you could shoot like that again with a musket?"

"A musket!"

Echohawk glanced at Glickihigan, who was smiling back at him. "I have shot my father's musket before," he said loudly.

"Brother-in-law, how did your son do with your musket?"

"Once he learned how to shoot it, his eye has never failed," Glickihigan said proudly. "I already told him this, Echohawk, before you were invited here tonight."

"A long time ago we stopped killing whites who came into our valley without asking." Tanebao Sachem shrugged his shoulders. "It does no good to kill them—more keep coming in every spring. As they come in, the deer leave. We need a hunter whose eye never fails. Echohawk, you will be that hunter."

The sachem motioned to Glickihigan, who stood near the door flap and shook out a bearskin in front of them.

The bearskin was huge; it covered half the wigwam floor. The great limbs were so long, one of the paws flopped into Echohawk's lap. He picked up the paw with both hands and couldn't see his own hands under it.

"We have decided to trade this bearskin for a musket for you, my son," Glickihigan said. "I will take you to *Saratoga-on-the-Hudson* before the winter moons."

Tenderly, Glickihigan touched the fiery left side of Echohawk's face. "Go home. Go to sleep," he said softly. "Do you understand? Makwa is a clan leader. I am not. He claimed the pride of the Bear clan was lost."

"His pride," Echohawk said bitterly. "Makwa has shown his anger to me, so who has won?"

"Who do you think?"

It took ten suns to skin the fifteen deer and roast and dry the venison. The women and girls tanned the hides over smoky fires to make clothes and blankets for the long winter ahead.

The next few suns it rained. Rainsong murmured against the bark of the wigwams from dawntime to sundown, and the clans stayed inside, stoking their starfires.

The next dawntime broke bright and clear. The rain had washed the smoke away from the camp, and the air smelled sweet and fresh.

"Bamaineo," Glickihigan said, "after morning corn I will take your brother to *Saratoga-on-the-Hudson*. We will return by sundown of the fourth sun. You will eat and sleep with the Wolf clan. They are expecting you."

"I will come back here to watch the starfire every morning and evening," Bamaineo said, frowning. "But why must I stay here? I never get to do anything."

"Next time you may go," Glickihigan promised.

After morning corn Echohawk and Glickihigan started walking. They took turns carrying the heavy bearskin so they had to stop and rest frequently, eating dried venison and ground parched corn from their waist pouches instead of taking the time to light a fire.

They slept by the Muhekunetuk that night and woke before the dawntime to get an early start. They walked without speaking until the sun was high above them.

"We will cross here. At the rapids," Glickihigan said. "The English have a camp for their warriors at the next bend of the Muhekunetuk."

They forded the rapids and rested while their leggings dried over a fire. For noon corn, they ate more corn and a rabbit Echohawk had shot and roasted two days before.

When they reached the next bend, Echohawk saw a fortress on the east bank of the river. It was the biggest building he'd ever seen, as big as their camp by the waterfall. Logs had been stacked one on top of the other, with big guns poking out of the ramparts. Echohawk had heard of these guns—*cannons*. Men were carrying logs, hauling water, washing clothes in the river, marching in formation.

Men in bright-red coats stood stiffly in front of the fort. The men were holding muskets.

Glickihigan looked directly at the men across the river and nodded to them, so Echohawk did the same. The men nodded back.

"What is the name of this warrior camp?" Echohawk asked.

"It is called *Fort Edward*. It is more like an English camp, though. The warriors' wives and children are inside. Their ways are different from ours. Among the English, a wife leaves her family and joins her husband's family."

"Strange," Echohawk said. "Father, at the deer hunt Tooksetuk told us he was leaving camp to get married. He will join his wife in Sokoki country. He is fourteen winters, only two winters older than me."

"Yes. Nehjao said Tooksetuk's bride is just your age. I think that is too young, for both of them."

"How many winters were you, when you married?"

His father chuckled. "Older than Tooksetuk, Echohawk."

"Oh."

"A husband always marries into his wife's wigwam,

but there is no one in camp for our sons to marry. Tooksetuk is leaving. Soon Gahko will leave, and you, then Bamaineo. What will happen to us? To our camp? It doesn't bear thinking about.

"There was a time when I thought you and your brother might marry two of Makwa's daughters."

"That will never happen," Echohawk said shortly.

"Yes. You are right."

"I will never leave her wigwam. I do not want to leave."

"Of course you will want to leave. So will Bamaineo. I will want my sons to leave and have families of their own."

"Then when Bamy marries, you and I will live with him. We will carry the turtle starfire with us in a stone pot."

Glickihigan shook his head. "Our starfires have been burning since the beginning, when the Creator, Kishelemukong, made the Great Turtle float up from the sea so the plants, the animals, and the People could live on his shell. What will happen when the starfires go out—"

When?

"—and the People die?" he asked sadly. "We must all try to live together on Great Turtle Island, but for us it is especially important. As long as even one of the People is alive, the Creator will not cause the Great Turtle to sink under the sea again. We must stay alive, because if we die, Great Turtle Island will die with us."

Echohawk only half listened, having heard the Great

Turtle story hundreds of times already. Instead, he imagined himself as a hawk, soaring high above Great Turtle Island. He looked down on the dense, quiet forests filled with game, the swift rivers filled with fish. Sunlight glittered on the Kipemapekan, the great fresh lakes. Prairie winds ruffled the grasslands, as wide as an ocean. He soared higher and flew over the shining mountains, then north again to the vast pine forests and finally to the icelands, even wider than the grasslands.

Forests, rivers, swamps, grasslands, mountains, deserts, glaciers, the animals, and the People—that Great Turtle Island could disappear forever filled him with horror and dread.

I will never let our starfire go out, Echohawk promised himself. *Since no one will marry me anyway, I will watch it for us. Forever.*

"My son, now you are wondering if you will ever have a wife."

Echohawk stopped in his tracks. "You always know what I am thinking," he said, his face hot with embarrassment. "I should no longer be surprised."

"You will be a good husband. You are kind, you care about your family, you are the best hunter I have ever seen. You must not worry—I will find you a good wife."

Echohawk shook his head. "They will all look into my white face and say no."

Glickihigan cupped his hands around Echohawk's face. "Those who say no are not worth having."

They walked on for a while before his father pointed

54

downstream. "Do you see that little island up ahead? That is the island before *Saratoga-on-the-Hudson*. Our sister the river is showing us the way"

They passed the island and took a steep deer trail straight up the riverbank to a road. They passed two log cabins, brand-new, one bigger than the other. The smaller cabin had a barn attached to it. A short time later they approached a little town.

The town! Echohawk looked around him eagerly. Some of the houses, stores, and mills were brand-new. Others were burned to the ground. People rushed down the main street with arms full of new wood and stones from the river. Others swarmed over log cabins, rebuilding the walls and restoring doors and roofs.

"They have worked hard to rebuild this camp," Glickihigan said. "They will have to work harder before the winter moons."

"What happened here, Father?"

"At the last Moon of Fallen Leaves, French and Hurons swept down the Muhekunetuk and burned this camp. They killed thirty people and took one hundred captives back to the Canadas with them. This is why I did not want Bamaineo to come with us. I did not know what we would see here."

"Why would the French and Hurons burn this camp?"

"The French think this is their country. The English think the same. They are like two bears fighting over the same blackberry bush."

"But this is *our* country."

"We are the blackberry bush." Glickihigan smiled. "Luke Warner has rebuilt. That is good." He pointed to a large log cabin at the far end of *Saratoga-on-the-Hudson*. "We are going there."

"Father, why did the warriors at *Fort Edward* not stop the French and Hurons?"

"That is a good question. It was at night, the moon was down. It was cold, and the English were inside sleeping under piles of blankets. A Frenchman is as noisy as any other white man, but the Hurons and their canoes are silent. The warriors neither saw nor heard them."

Luke Warner's cabin was bigger than the rest and had a wide porch in front. White men were sitting on chairs eyeing the new arrivals curiously. Glickihigan stepped up to the front door.

"Hello!" Glickihigan shouted.

"Come in," a voice shouted from the inside.

They entered the trading place.

A white man stood in the center of the building. His bright-red hair and beard surrounded his face like fire. Echohawk watched carefully as Luke Warner placed his right hand in front of him and held it toward Glickihigan, as though to give him something. But his hand was empty. Glickihigan touched his palm to Luke Warner's palm and they curled their fingers around each other's hands, like an animal trap.

Why would they trap each other's hands that way? Echohawk thought. But soon his attention was caught by all the goods around him. Some of the things he recognized—bolts of cloth, needles and thread, iron axeheads, mirrors, glass beads and jars, shot and powder, cooking pots, forks and spoons. His father had been trading furs for the white man's goods for as long as he could remember. Other things, with their odd shapes and textures, he could only stare at and wonder.

Echohawk touched the side of something made of stiff, black cloth. It was triangular in shape, like a cottonwood leaf.

"Father, what is this?" he asked, turning toward the men.

But Glickihigan was unfolding the bearskin and spreading it on the counter with a flourish. The great arms and legs, the claws the size of a man's fingers, hung to the floor. Glickihigan brushed the thick fur against the grain to make the hair stand up again. He lifted two of the paws.

Luke Warner's eyes grew bigger and bigger. He and Echohawk's father talked back and forth for a few moments before Luke Warner walked to the back of the trading place. He disappeared behind a buckskin hanging on the wall.

"How could he disappear into the wall? Where did he go?" Echohawk asked.

"The inside of a white man's home is called a *room*. He has another *room* behind this one." Glickihigan picked up the triangular object. "You were asking about this. It is called a *hat*, a *tricornered hat*."

He put the tricornered hat on Echohawk's head.

The hat fell around Echohawk's ears and rested on the bridge of his nose. "I am not supposed to see anything?"

"It is too big for you. A round face under the triangular shape is pleasing to the eye." Glickihigan put the hat on his head. "There, am I pleasing to the eye?"

Echohawk laughed. "You look different."

Luke Warner came back holding four muskets. Glickihigan put the tricornered hat down and motioned for Echohawk to come to the counter. "I have told Luke Warner that my son needs a musket."

"This is your son, is he?"

Luke Warner smiled into Echohawk's face. His smile turned to puzzlement as he looked at the tall young man dressed in deerskin standing solemnly in front of him. Echohawk's long, brown hair hung in waves to his waist, his eyes were yellow-brown, and his skin was white along the undersides of his arms and chin.

"He's . . . your son?"

"I have told him, Echohawk, that I have never seen anyone with such keen eyesight or steady hands. The deer and moose are becoming hard to find. You need a musket so you can hunt for our People."

"What's your name, boy?"

Luke Warner put his hand out. His eyes were the bright gray color of woodsmoke as it drifts through sunshine. When Echohawk, imitating Glickihigan's earlier action, grasped Luke Warner's hand, he was surprised at how soft it was. It felt like one of Bamaineo's hands when he had been a baby.

Glickihigan picked up the longest musket and gave it his son. When Echohawk set the stock on the floor, the musket's barrel came up over his head.

Luke Warner laughed, shook his head, and said something.

"Luke Warner says this musket is taller than you and much too heavy. He says you will not be able to hold it steady enough. Show him," Glickihigan said, a smile playing on his lips.

Echohawk's arms were strong. He held the musket up to his shoulder and looked through the sight. The long rifle didn't move.

Out of the corner of his eye, Echohawk saw Luke Warner staring at him with the same look he'd had for the bearskin. He set the musket on the counter, and Glickihigan nodded to Luke Warner.

The shop owner fumbled with a glass jar on a shelf, then handed something to Echohawk.

Echohawk had never seen such a thing. It was smooth like a bone and had red and white stripes on it like war paint.

"Put it in your mouth, Echohawk."

"Why?"

"Because it is food. Go on, it is polite."

Echohawk put one end in his mouth. It tasted like a mint leaf.

"It is a *peppermint stick*. My son," Glickihigan said softly, "our best cooking pots and spoons are buried with her. You choose some more, ones you and your brother will like."

BEFORE THEY LEFT FOR HOME, they sat down on the porch outside the tavern to drink cold cider. Echohawk tried to study everything at once. Some of the women had shining yellow hair the color of corn silk, some had brownish-red hair like the color of water stained with autumn leaves. Their hair curled around their faces like grapevines.

Some of the men wore bright-red coats like the ones at *Fort Edward*. Echohawk always wore strips of bright cloth tied below his knees to keep his leggings in place. But their black leggings were so stiff, they stood up by themselves.

There was a white man's face painted on a piece of wood hanging above the tavern door. *That man must be the totem of this camp,* Echohawk thought.

"What is the name of their totem here?" He nodded toward the painting.

"He is not their totem, Echohawk. He is their sachem. *George* Sachem. His father was also named *George*. That

61

is *George* Sachem the Second. He is your sachem; mine too. But say nothing about this to Tanebao Sachem or you will hurt his feelings."

"Where have you met this sachem?"

"He lives across the Sun's Salt Sea, but he is sachem to all of us, even those who live far to the south in the Land That Is Never Cold."

As Echohawk studied the painting, he noticed that the tavern walls were made of stones. Stones from the river! How did the stones stand on top of one another and not fall down?

Everywhere there were log cabins, built straight up and down like the lodges of the Iroquois. Everyone was talking at once, like squirrels in the trees!

Glickihigan covered Echohawk's hand with his. "Do not look around so much," he said in a low voice. "You are making these white men nervous."

Just then a little panther jumped on their table. Echohawk lunged back on the bench. In a flash he had his tomahawk out. Instantly the men on the tavern porch stood up and faced Echohawk. Some had their pistols drawn.

"Wait," his father whispered softly. "Put your tomahawk away slowly. Watch what she does."

Instead of lunging at their throats, the little black animal sat on its haunches and began washing its front paws.

"Why are their panthers so small?"

"Echohawk, she is not a panther. She is a *cat*."

Glickihigan repeated the English word again. *"Cat."*

Glickihigan shouted something to the men in English. They all laughed, sat down, and put their pistols away. Glickihigan reached out and stroked behind the cat's ears.

"Try it. She will not hurt you."

Echohawk touched the cat along her shoulders. He'd never touched a living animal before. Her smooth muscles shifted under her warm fur. She purred and arched against his hand before jumping down from the table. Echohawk watched her trot lightly to a far corner under the tavern wall.

I can see what a panther's den looks like.

Softly, Echohawk walked to the far corner of the tavern.

The cat was licking four newborn cubs that were mewing to her and kneading their paws into her soft stomach. They were all purring. The purring noise rose like heat to his ears.

As Echohawk came closer, the cubs stopped climbing over their mother and became still. They didn't make a sound. They were as quiet and still as stones as he approached.

Echohawk frowned. Silent panther cubs? No, there was another word for these cubs. Echohawk searched his memory but couldn't think of the word.

As he stared at the cat family, his heart started pounding. His skin turned cold, and his chest and stomach knotted in terror. The muscles in his arms and legs trembled violently like snakes racing under his skin.

Why? Why would I be afraid of a tiny panther and her cubs? Silent panther cubs as quiet as stones.

Smoke, fire, screaming—

"We should leave soon. If we hurry, we will be home by sundown tomorrow. Echohawk?" Glickihigan stood next to him.

"What is the name of this animal?" Echohawk asked in a shaky voice.

"Cat," Glickihigan replied.

"And her cubs?"

His father frowned, trying to remember. *"Kittens. They are called kittens."*

The dimmest edge of memory was just beyond his grasp. *"Kittens.* I wish I could remember." The kittens, no longer afraid, were mewing and crawling over their mother again. The memory, or the memory of the memory, was gone.

"You are trembling," Glickihigan said. "What is wrong?"

"I—I want to go home," Echohawk replied. "I want to show Bamy my musket and tell him about the white man's camp. I want to see his face when he puts the mint stick in his mouth."

On the way upriver Echohawk was quiet, watching his moccasined feet walking beneath him. His musket was heavy and his arm muscles began to ache. The breeze from the river was not a hot, muggy summer breeze that gave no relief. This breeze was a cool, autumn one, blowing down from the Canadas. It made him feel, of all things, thirsty.

"*Saratoga-on-the-Hudson,*" Glickihigan said. "Now you have many questions about yourself."

Echohawk caught his breath, then laughed. "You always know what I am thinking. You are right. I have many questions.

"I have heard this story so many times, Father. You found me hiding in a log. I had been sick, I was so terrified. But terrified of what? What was I hiding from? Where was this log? Why was I all by myself? What—what happened to me?"

The Muhekunetuk was a deep-blue shadow in the slanting afternoon sunshine. The birches, already yellow with the approaching autumn, were lit up brilliant gold at the very top of the riverbanks.

"Another summer over," Glickihigan said. "Those birch trees are the color of sunshine. Look." He pointed at the birches. "You remember nothing?" he asked softly, standing behind his son.

"I remember nothing. Can you tell me anything more?"

"No," Glickihigan said quickly. "Except this log you speak of was far south of here. You were very little—we guessed you were four winters, maybe less. I carried you all the way to the camp. You were like a stone. Before you came into your name, she called you Bear Cub because sometimes a mother bear hides her cubs in hollow logs. Do you remember that?"

Echohawk had a sudden, vivid image of himself waking up, sitting bolt upright on his sleeping platform and screaming, screaming! His mother scooping him up and holding him close. "My frightened little Bear Cub, such a frightened little Bear Cub, it is all right, just a dream, just a dream," his mother had crooned in his ear again and again. He could hardly hear her for the screaming.

"Breeze of Summer, he can sleep with us tonight," his father had said. There had been something odd about his father's face. As though . . . as though . . . what?

As though he knew what I was thinking. That is nothing new.

Echohawk thought carefully about the memory. He saw the scene again in his mind's eye. He felt, again, his heart pounding in terror and the warmth of the starfire on his back. He smelled again the sweet, smoky smell of his mother's shoulder as she held him.

His father's face.

There was something else—concern and love and something hidden, private. *As though . . . as though he knew what I was* dreaming, *too. No, I must be mistaken.*

Kitten stones?

Glickihigan's quiet, unreadable face pointed westward. He was still looking at the birch trees on the far riverbank.

"Why did you call her Breeze of Summer?" Echohawk asked shyly. "That was not her name."

Windsong, he thought. How he wanted to say her name out loud! *Windsong, Windsong.*

66

"Breeze of Summer," his father said softly, "because her voice was cool and gentle and always welcome." He put his hand on the back of Echohawk's head. "Bamaineo is waiting."

"She called my brother Honeybee. He has always seemed to me to be more of a honeybee than a bounding elk."

Glickihigan smiled. "Your brother loves honey, and he sticks to you as though you are a bear cub with honey smeared on your chest. He will come into his name. You must call him Bamaineo now, and he will come into his name sooner. He will be like a bounding elk."

Echohawk hesitated. "I would like to talk about her. I think about her from the time I wake up until the time I go to sleep. I dream about her at night. It would hurt less to talk about her."

"We never talk about her because she is not gone," his father said sternly. "She is in the circle of time."

"But if she is not gone, then what difference—"

"No. You will not repeat either of her names. She is not gone," Glickihigan repeated hoarsely.

"Bamaineo would also like to talk about our mother." The last two words were barely a whisper.

"You were so frightened, those first few moons. You learned to trust her, Echohawk. And by trusting her, you learned to trust the rest of us. That is all I am going to say."

They started walking again.

"Father, where did you learn English?"

"*Albany*. I learned to speak and read English, how to count *money*. We read from the whites' stories of their spirits called the *Bible*. The camp of my boyhood, Schodac, is near *Albany*. Everyone in Schodac is *Christian* now. They wear the white man's clothes. I no longer know my own people. They have already forgotten so many things.

"I was your brother's age when my father sent me. *Albany* then was the size of *Saratoga-on-the-Hudson* now. My father learned Dutch as a boy, but he could see the English growing stronger than they. It was good I learned English instead."

Glickihigan stopped walking and looked at Echohawk in surprise.

"Now *I* can ask *you* what is wrong."

"I have forgotten something," Glickihigan said. "Something important."

Echohawk was grinning back at him. "I am going to name my musket 'Thunderpath.' Thank you for trading for him, Father."

CHAPTER SEVEN

ECHOHAWK STEPPED INTO the turtle wigwam with three naahmao in his belt.

"Look what Echohawk has," Bamaineo shouted.

"Father," Echohawk said, his eyes shining as he laid two of the wild turkeys at Glickihigan's feet, "I have shot these with my new musket. I will give the third one to our sachem."

"Tanebao Sachem will like that. You are ready for your Vision Quest," Glickihigan said softly. "You will start tomorrow."

Echohawk swallowed hard. "I am ready."

He sat down next to Bamaineo by the starfire and folded his arms tightly.

My Vision Quest, he thought. *Before my thirteenth winter, four days and three nights with no food, water, weapons, or clothes. It begins tomorrow. Just like that.*

"Perhaps you are both thinking about Makwako," their father said. Bamaineo's eyes were as big as an owl's. "It is impossible to say what happened to

Makwa's oldest son, why he never returned from his Vision Quest. But Tooksetuk came back. He came back a man and a warrior. I came back. My spirit-helper revealed herself and my future to me."

"Herself?" Echohawk exclaimed. "Your spirit-helper is . . . a—a female animal?"

"Yes," Glickihigan said simply. "Now is the best time, Echohawk, before the winter moons. Bamaineo, you can pluck and clean these turkeys, and I will roast them."

"Why do I have to pluck and clean them?" Bamaineo grumbled.

"Because you did not hunt them."

The next morning Echohawk went down to the river while his family ate their morning corn. He tried not to think about the roasted turkey from the night before.

I am already hungry. Stop, he told himself sternly. *You have not even started fasting yet.* He thought he could hear the waterfall upriver, whispering in his ears. Taunting him.

His father joined him at the riverbank. "I will walk with you to the waterfall," Glickihigan said.

The waterfall was north of the camp. Echohawk had seen it a thousand times while swimming or on hunting trips, but this time, as they stood on the riverbank next to it, the crashing water seemed to be laughing at him, teasing him.

Echohawk took off his moccasins and breechcloth

and gave them to his father. No one ever swam this close to the waterfall. The pounding water and hidden rocks were much too dangerous.

Water tumbled over the falls and roared in his ears.

"Tooksetuk said there is a rock shelf on the other side of the falls where we are supposed to stand," he shouted.

His father nodded. "This is to make you strong, pure, to show Manitou how much you want your Vision. When I hold my hand up like this, that is your signal to come back. Be strong!"

Echohawk dove underwater. He expected to see the shelf on the far side of the waterfall; he had seen that rock shelf a hundred times in his mind. But the tumbling water continued to fall through the river, hiding everything underneath it in a cliff of white.

What do I do now? he thought.

He came to the surface and filled his lungs with air. Swimming underwater again, he felt along the far edge of the waterfall until he found the rock ledge. He climbed onto the ledge and, taking another deep breath, walked backward into the waterfall.

Be strong!

But the cold water thundered in his ears and pounded the top of his head and shoulders. He locked his knees to keep them from buckling. He was standing right under the crashing water. It was impossible to breathe or see. Water rushed into his mouth, nose, and eyes. Occasionally a falling fish hit his shoulders and neck with the force of a rock. He cupped his hands over his nose and mouth so he could breathe.

One, two, three, four, five, Echohawk counted. He ducked his head out of the crashing water and quickly glanced at Glickihigan. *Not yet. One, two, three, four, five*—his father still hadn't raised his hand. *How much longer? One*—

He felt ashamed. This was the first step and all he could think about was when it would be over! He told himself to ignore the pain, to see it but not feel it. To ignore the pain was to have power over it. The sort of power that comes with honor. Echohawk closed his eyes and thought hard about his Vision.

When he looked again, his father was waving both hands above his head and shouting. Echohawk dove into the river and swam toward him. His head and shoulders hurt from the pounding water and his hearing had a hollowness to it, as though his ears were stuffed with corn silk.

He stood on the riverbank dripping water.

"There are those who are saying you can have no Vision, that you are not able to have one," Glickihigan said loudly.

"I have heard them say this," Echohawk shouted back above the thundering water.

"I know you will have a great Vision. I am certain of it. But having a Vision and having the understanding of it are two different things," Glickihigan shouted. "It is not uncommon to live years and years without the understanding. This happened to me."

Glickihigan cupped his hands around his son's wet face.

"How very strange life is, that your life and mine are on the same path." He studied Echohawk's face, as though burning it into his memory. Then he pressed his forehead against his son's for an instant. "You were in my Vision," he said quickly. "A wolf mother, fierce, guarding her two young ones. One of the cubs was a fox."

Echohawk's jaw dropped open as his father turned away.

"No one sees you now," he shouted. "You are with the spirits."

Glickihigan walked away without looking back, not even once.

Echohawk felt small and weak without his weapons and clothes. He headed upriver and turned north, away from *Saratoga-on-the-Hudson*.

Just in case they don't know I am invisible, he thought, grinning to himself.

First, look for a good place for my Vision.

It felt good to be looking for something and not just wandering naked in the woods.

The entire first sun was spent looking and waiting for a sign that he was looking in the right place.

He tore branches off a cedar tree and used them to cover himself the first night. In the dawntime, when the mosquitoes were hungriest, Echohawk stayed huddled under the branches even though he was eager to begin looking again, because mosquitoes hate the smell of cedar.

His stomach was growling, and his lips and mouth were dry. He tried hard not to think about food, but whenever he closed his eyes, favorite dishes appeared before him. Corn bread with maple syrup, roasted duck with the rich fat still under the crackling skin, smoked venison, roasted turkey, his mother's corn cakes with wild cherries, sassafras tea, cool water—

"Stop!"

He sat up. The second sun.

Today I find my Vision Place.

Echohawk walked north again. His head buzzed, as though a swarm of bees were following him. His vision would darken suddenly, then stars would float around the edges. Sunlight hurt his eyes and head, so he stayed in the deep forest.

At dusk he tore off more cedar branches and huddled under them. He had prayed to Manitou all day and had not seen anything that looked like a Vision Place. *Tomorrow I will find it,* he promised himself. He curled under the branches and tried to sleep.

On the morning of the third sun, his tongue felt like wood, his mouth as dry as ashes. When he stood up, his legs wobbled, and the buzzing in his head was even louder.

All he could think about was water. Water! Swimming in the Muhekunetuk and drinking as much cold, clean water as he wanted. His lips were cracked and the sun was already so hot.

He picked up his cedar branches and forced himself to walk.

Manitou, show me something today, the Vision Place, the Vision, something. He took a deep breath and prayed to the Creator, Kishelemukong, too. *Kishelemukong, please.*

Hot sunlight felt like arrows in his eyes, and his head ached. The buzzing was even louder now.

At noon he heard yipping and yelping and long howls. Wolves! Echohawk turned around in terror, expecting to see a pack of hungry wolves behind him. There were no wolves.

The sunlight in the forest was greenish and shimmering. Echohawk imagined the forest was underwater and he was walking on the riverbed, far away from the wolves. How good it would feel to be underwater! Even standing under the waterfall again would be better than this.

Branches and brambles scratched him all over, and the salt from his dried sweat and blood made the scratches sting.

Most of the trees along the riverbank were so big, a man could put his arms around one and not be able to touch his hands together on the other side. The blue sky was hidden by the mighty trees, their branches tangled together like the roof of a wigwam far above his head.

So Echohawk was surprised when he came upon a patch of new-growth forest. These trees were young, about as big around as one of his legs. Bushes grew alongside them. It made no sense for the new-growth trees to be there. The bright blue sky and the sun shone above him.

The wolves were back.

The yips, yelps, and howls were louder and more urgent. The buzzing grew to a roar. But instead of running away from the wolves, he wanted to stay in the bright new-growth forest, to see what would happen there. *This is the place,* he thought, his heart pounding in excitement. *Thank you, Manitou, for showing me my Vision Place. Kishelemukong? Thank you.*

He covered himself with cedar branches and sat down to wait. He fell asleep to the sound of wolves howling, each wolf howling his own note but in harmony with his neighbor.

Echohawk woke with a start. It was late morning. He'd slept through too much of the fourth sun. His last sun! He would have to go home today, whether he had a Vision or not.

He leaned against one of the new-growth trees and stared hard at the slim trees around him. There were patches of summer blue sky between the green leaves. The green leaves and the blue sky seemed to bend, to sway forward and backward in front of him.

Hunger and thirst hurt. His stomach felt as though he'd swallowed hot knives, and his dry tongue stuck to the roof of his mouth. His head pounded with pain, and his saltless muscles shook with pain. His skin hurt. It hurt to stand and make water. It hurt just to open his eyes. It hurt to think.

Water and salt, I need water and salt. Smoked fish, smoked venison, corn stew with salty ashes stirred into it . . .

As he thought of all his favorite salty foods, the leaves and sky swayed in front of him. He swayed too. The green of the leaves and the blue of the sky pulled him forward, then pushed him back. Summer heat pounded on the top of his head like the waterfall.

Green and blue, water and salt, green and blue, water and salt: a chant, a quiet dance in his head. He forgot about his pain—the chant cleared his mind.

His thinking felt light, as though his head were a feather that would float away at the first strong breeze.

Green and blue . . . he swayed forward. *Water and salt* . . . he swayed back. Chanting, he swayed forward and backward all afternoon.

Green and blue, water and salt, green and blue, water and salt, green and gray: the sky was gray. It was dusk of the fourth sun and there had been no Vision.

Thick tears stung his eyes, and his breathing came in dry sobs. "Makwa and Gahko are right," he cried. "I can have no Vision."

He put his face in his hands. The buzzing came back, the yipping, yelping, and howling came back. "Come and get me then," he cried out. He threw a handful of pine needles at the howling.

"How can I go back to camp with no Vision?"

The evening wind picked up. The leaves were moving. No, the gray sky between the leaves was moving. The gray sky compressed, thickened, and became shapes. The long gray shapes were moving, but running in place, because they always stayed in front of him. The yipping, yelping, and howling moved closer.

Wolves.

Running. A pack of wolves was running.

He held his breath and didn't dare move a muscle.

The fastest wolf ran out in front of the rest and sank his teeth into the leg of a deer. As the deer fell, the wolf turned his head toward Echohawk. His eyes were yellow-brown. A message pushed through the air from the wolf and into Echohawk's heart: The wolf was himself.

The wolf dropped the deer, opened his mouth, and grinned at Echohawk. His yellow-brown eyes sparkled in pleasure.

"I have found you, brother," he said to Echohawk. "And I have been looking and looking."

As the rest of the wolves caught up, the fastest wolf turned toward Echohawk again and shot forward. His strides became longer and longer.

Echohawk held his arms out toward the wolf. *Yes. You have found me. You are my spirit-helper, the hawk, my spirit-brother. The wolf and the hawk, I understand. How good it is you have found me.*

The wolf grinned.

An older wolf and a much younger one tried to follow the fastest wolf, but they soon melted into the gray sky between the leaves.

No! Wait for them. Wait.

The wolf's strides lengthened. The paws were no longer on the ground. The wolf was flying.

The wolf's back legs became claws, his front legs became wings, his soft gray fur became hard brown feathers. From wolf to hawk: Everything changed but the yellow-brown eyes.

The hawk swooped forward, his fierce face a hand's width from Echohawk. His feathers beat into Echohawk's face. Both cried out at the same time. The back of Echohawk's head hit the tree, and the hawk, trees, and sky became as the night.

When he woke, the gray was just sky between the leaves again. The forest was silent. Was it dusk or dawntime? Day or night? It was impossible to know.

It was impossible to get up, crushed by such a deep sadness. For Echohawk knew exactly what his Vision meant.

Wolves hunt and live in packs.
Hawks hunt and live alone.

"Echohawk's back," Bamaineo shouted at the same moment his brother fell through the door flap and onto the wigwam floor.

"I have water ready for you," Glickihigan said. He sat Echohawk up against a sleeping platform and brought a bowl to his lips. "We have waited all night for you to come back."

"Water," Echohawk whispered.

"Here. One sip now, two sips in a little while, three sips after that. Morning corn later."

Echohawk gulped and felt the cool water wash through his body in a wave.

"And salt," he whispered.

CHAPTER EIGHT

THE SUN KICKED OFF HIS NIGHT BLANKET later and later, so the mornings were darker and colder. With their father gone again, Echohawk and Bamaineo decided to bring the sleeping mats in from the summer porch.

In the dawntime they woke to the sound of thousands of birds calling to one another along the riverbank and in the forest. The birds crowded the tree branches, the thin ends of the branches sagging almost to the river with their weight. The birdsong was so loud, the brothers couldn't speak to each other unless one shouted right into the other's ear.

Entire flocks of birds swooped down into the trees, calling to their own kind for the long journey south. The birds flew from tree to tree, marsh to marsh, sorting themselves out. Robins in that oak, bluebirds in that ash tree, thousands of golden finches turning the blueberry bushes bright yellow with their feathers.

When the birds were gathered by kind, they would rest silently for a moment, gathering strength. Then they would burst from the trees in huge waves of flapping wings. They flew downriver, blocking out the sun. During morning corn, Echohawk could hold out his hand and lose his own shadow against the floor of the summer porch.

The coming winter meant a lot of work for the clans. There were the Sacred Sisters to harvest: the corn, the squash, and the beans. The Sacred Sisters were kept in the storehouse along with the smoked fish and venison from the deer hunt. The clans used the same deep holes in the storehouse year after year, burying the vegetables in baskets in the ground so they would stay cold but not freeze.

The women and children picked as many wild berries and grapes as they could find. They would dry them in the sun, then pound them into bright red and purple dust. The berry dust was stored in brightly colored pots with close-fitting lids. The women would add the berry dust to winter stew pots.

Most of the corn was dried, ground into meal, then parched into nokekik. In the winter the nokekik was mixed with clean snow and baked into cakes around the starfire. They would eat these cakes with last year's maple sugar. If spring was very late and the stored food was gone, nokekik was all the clans ate until the ice broke and the snow melted.

When Glickihigan came home again, the clans were stacking pumpkins and squash in the storehouse.

"Glickihigan!" Bamaineo shouted from the pumpkin patch.

"Glickihigan!" Echohawk stepped out of the store-house to welcome his father home.

"My sons, come into the wigwam. I have something to tell you."

When they were settled around the starfire, their father started talking. "I have been to *Saratoga-on-the-Hudson* again"—he gave them each a peppermint stick—"because I forgot something important. It is past the time for my sons to learn English and the ways of our English neighbors. You both should have gone to *school* in *Saratoga-on-the-Hudson* a long time ago."

"We are going to live in *Saratoga-on-the-Hudson?*" Echohawk exclaimed. "The white man's camp?"

Bamaineo's peppermint stick fell right out of his mouth. The brothers looked at each other across the starfire.

"Echohawk, it is important for you to learn the ways of the people you were born to."

"I'm not—"

"Echohawk, someday you may feel a pull toward them. If that should happen, you must be ready for it."

"But I will not feel—"

"Bamaineo, your life to come will be very different from mine. You must be ready too.

"We will leave our camp in two suns. I have already spoken to your teacher, Mr. Joshua Warner, and his wife, Jerusha. I know his brother well, Luke Warner. He owns the trading place. Luke Warner is kind and can be trusted. We will trust his brother, Joshua.

"You will live with them for the winter. He is from a huge white man's camp by the Sun's Salt Sea, *Boston,* and he knows a lot about his people. He is a great shaman—a holy man. Now, what did you cook for today?"

"Makwasi taught us how to cook venison with cranberries," Echohawk replied. "Why do we have to—"

"That sounds good. We will eat now."

Two suns later, the Turtle clan picked up the turtle starfire log by log and added the logs to the wolf starfire. They took down the turtle wigwam and stacked the branches, bark, mats, and deerskins in the storehouse. They packed their winter clothes, long robes of deer and wolfskin, and their winter moccasins, made with the fur side in to keep their feet warm and dry. Their bearskin winter blankets, too, were folded and packed into the knapsacks.

Echohawk brought his musket, Thunderpath, with enough shot and powder to last the winter in case the white man's camp didn't store food the way the clans did.

They lashed their snowshoes onto the knapsacks last.

Their heads were so full of thoughts of *school* and town that Echohawk and Bamaineo did not look behind them as they left their camp.

Now there were only three wigwams: the royal turtle wigwam of Tanebao Sachem, and the wolf and the bear. The storehouse faced the community firepit, where the fish had been dried. Behind it lay the empty cornfield and the pumpkin and squash patch. There were now seventeen people in the camp where once there had been hundreds. Fifty clans with ten wigwams each had stretched along the banks of the Muhekunetuk.

Echohawk, Bamaineo, and Glickihigan walked down the riverbank in single file, making slow progress because of all they were carrying with them.

"Tell me about the white man's camp again, Echohawk," Bamaineo urged. "Tell me everything again."

"There is so much to say," Echohawk replied. "There was a huge longhouse made of stone."

"Why did the stones agree to stand on one another?"

"Maybe at night they roll home again to the riverbank."

Bamaineo shook his head. "It makes no sense—"

"The English had leggings like ours, but they were stiff and black like tree trunks. The leggings stood up by themselves."

"*Boots,*" Glickihigan said from behind them.

"Tell me about the trading place again. Where you traded for Thunderpath. Tell me about the tiny panther again."

"The trading place was so full, it looked like our storehouse does now. The tiny panther was gentle, friendly."

"*Cat,*" Glickihigan called out from behind.

"Will we live in a stone wigwam or a log wigwam, Echohawk?"

"All except one of their buildings were made of logs."

"Logs, then. Good. Because if the stones roll home to the riverbank every night, we would have no place to sleep. Tell me about the women again."

Echohawk stepped around a small rock pool. They had a long way to go and he didn't want wet feet.

"They are pretty," he said thoughtfully. "Their hair is yellow like corn silk, or brown like mine, or red like that tree." Echohawk pointed to a large sugar maple tree growing along the riverbank. Its leaves were fiery red against the brilliant blue sky.

"Do you know why the leaves turn bright red in autumn, Echohawk?" Bamaineo asked.

"Another story, little brother?"

"We are now at the end of the Green Corn Moon. Soon we will mark the beginning of the Sky-Bears Moon. This time of year the bears are fighting over the best places to sleep for the winter. These best sleeping places are warm and dry and are hidden from us so we cannot find the bears while they sleep. Bears are smart; they remember where the best winter sleeping places are.

"The Sky-Bears are also looking for the best places to sleep for the winter. Sky-Bears are huge and there are very few caves and hollow trees in the sky. The Sky-Bears fight hard over the best sleeping places, biting with their sharp teeth and scratching with their claws as long and sharp as knives.

"As they fight, the Sky-Bears' blood falls to the earth and drips on the leaves. This is why the leaves turn red."

"A good story, Bamy."

"Echohawk?"

"Yes?"

"What if . . . what if the English want to kill us?"

Echohawk shook his head. "Our father has chosen our winter camp wisely. We will be living in the wigwam of their shaman. They will not hurt us there. Their spirits of the dead would be too angry."

"But what about when we are in *school*?"

"He is also the shaman of the *school*. We will be all right."

They walked all day, making a small camp that night.

For evening corn they ate nokekik so they wouldn't have to make a fire. They mixed the parched corn with river water and ate it from their hands.

The next day they crossed at the rapids and changed into dry leggings and moccasins. They walked past *Fort Edward* and stopped for noon corn, nokekik again, Bamaineo chattering like a squirrel with questions about the fort.

It was late afternoon when they came upon the island before the town. They walked up a steep deer trail.

First was the school yard, an empty field as big as their vegetable garden at home. Echohawk remembered the large log cabin in front of it. *So that's the school*, he thought. Next was a smaller building with a barn attached; the barn was the same size as the schoolhouse. School, house, and barn looked out over the river. All three buildings were brand new.

"Mr. Joshua Warner," Glickihigan shouted as they reached the clearing. "Mrs. Jerusha Warner."

A tall older man dressed in black came out of the cabin and stood on the porch. His lips were pinched together, like the mouth of a grapevine net when it is drawn tight and full of fish. Next to him stood a younger woman in a plain brown dress.

"Her hair *is* like corn silk," Bamaineo whispered.

"I told you," Echohawk whispered back.

Bamaineo tried to hide behind him as they walked toward the schoolmaster and his wife. "No," Echohawk said firmly. He pulled his brother from behind and pushed him forward. "Your fear will only make them stronger."

"Mr. Glickihigan." Mr. Warner reached down and shook hands with their father. He said something, and Glickihigan answered in a pleasant voice. Mrs. Warner talked to Glickihigan, then nodded to the brothers.

"They want to meet you," Glickihigan whispered. He pushed Echohawk and Bamaineo forward.

"Watch carefully, little brother. You must do exactly the same thing."

Echohawk put his hand in front of him. As Mr. Warner shook hands, he peered into Echohawk's face. The schoolmaster's eyes widened in surprise.

"Bamaineo," Glickihigan said, "do not be afraid."

Bamaineo stepped forward and put his hand out so fast, he hit Mr. Warner right in the stomach.

Mr. Warner jumped. "Bamaineo," he said with an

embarrassed laugh. As he shook Bamaineo's hand, he studied Echohawk again.

Mrs. Warner picked up her skirts and walked into the house. Mr. Warner followed.

Even as the cabin door closed behind them, Bamaineo was speaking. "If we do not like the English camp, when can we go home?"

"I am not going back to our camp. You must stay here for the winter, Bamaineo," Glickihigan replied. "I will travel west, through Iroquois country, to the Ohio River. The trapping is still good there, and the Delaware are our grandfathers and fathers. I will stay with them."

"Iroquois country," Echohawk exclaimed. "Our blood enemies! If they capture you, they will kill you!"

"I will be careful," his father replied. "Their country is huge and I will not be there for long.

"Echohawk, you are almost as tall as I am. When we see each other again, perhaps you will be taller than I. I know you will take good care of your little brother."

Echohawk felt his throat and chest tighten. He pressed his lips together to keep them from trembling.

"Good-bye, Father," he whispered quickly.

Bamaineo was wiping his eyes with a deerskin sleeve.

Glickihigan knelt in front of him. "Bamaineo, don't be afraid—no one will hurt you here. What moon is this?"

"The Green Corn Moon," he cried into his father's shoulder.

"And in two suns?"

"Sky-Bears. Iroquois country!"

"Before you go to sleep tonight, look at the moon. He is not quite full. When he looks like that again before the Sugar Maple Moon, I will come back for you. Bamaineo, I know you will do everything Echohawk tells you to do. While I am gone, you will hear my voice in his."

Glickihigan stood up and drew the boys close to him.

"Learn English as fast as you can. Practice every day. You will need this English in your future even more than I needed it in mine.

"Do everything the shaman and his wife say. You will not understand much of what they want you to do. Do it anyway. Remember you are Turtle clan. That makes us special, because a turtle can live both on land *and* in water. I know you can live here for the winter.

"Go inside. Remember, two suns before the Sugar Maple Moon."

"I promise," Echohawk said. He nudged Bamaineo with his foot.

"I promise, too," Bamaineo cried.

Glickihigan knelt down to pick up his musket and pack. Echohawk had never noticed before the gray hair woven into the black in his father's braids.

"One more thing," Glickihigan said to Echohawk as he stood up. "I told them your name is *Jonathan.*"

"Why did you tell them that?"

But their father turned away quickly and walked

across the clearing to the deer trail. He didn't look behind him, not even once.

"What did he say about your name?"

"Stop crying, Bamy. My name is Echohawk."

CHAPTER NINE

"JONATHAN! BAMAINEO!" the brothers heard from below. It was Mrs. Warner, shouting at them in the early morning.

Echohawk and Bamaineo sat up with a start. They were in the attic of the Warners' house. Sunshine slipped in through the cracks in the log wall and dappled across the quilts, their clothes, and the floor.

"Echohawk! Where are we?" Bamaineo exclaimed. "How can she be shouting below us?"

"Because she *is* below us. This wigwam is like a tree; we can climb higher and higher in it. You fell asleep last night. I carried you up here.

"Look." Echohawk punched the mattress. "Guess what's inside. Corn husks!"

"But how did—"

"Look." Echohawk pointed to the top of a ladder leaning against the landing. "That is like a tree's branches. We can climb up here at night."

"Jonathan! Bamaineo!" Mrs. Warner called again.

92

"She has cooked something for morning corn," Echohawk said. "Are you as hungry as I am?"

"I really have to go. We have to go to the woods first."

They climbed down the ladder and ran out the back door. When they returned, Jerusha Warner pointed to a bowl full of water for washing their hands. As they washed, she laid out a meal for them: ham, eggs, fried apples and cinnamon, flapjacks with maple syrup, mashed sweet potatoes with ham gravy, and mugs of strong tea.

Bamaineo had not eaten since the nokekik from the day before, and he gobbled down his food as though he were starved.

"Bamy," Echohawk whispered across the table to him. "Do not eat so quickly. They are looking at you. Perhaps that is rude."

Mr. Warner stood up so fast, he knocked his chair over. It landed with a *thud* on the dirt floor. He shouted at Echohawk while Mrs. Warner tugged at her husband's sleeve.

What did I do? Why is he so angry? Echohawk said to himself.

Mr. Warner seized the brothers by their shirts and marched them across the clearing and into the school yard. The school yard was full of students. Town girls skipped rope or played tag, and the boys played stickball or teased the girls.

Most of the students were from the town, but some were from neighboring tribes. Echohawk recognized the

93

tightly braided hair of the Sokoki and the long arms and legs of the Abenaki. On the far edge of the school yard, some Mohawks stood by themselves. Their gazes met and clashed.

When the students saw the Reverend Mr. Warner, they dropped their games and ran into the schoolhouse.

The reason became clear. They all grabbed seats along the back benches and the wall. By the time Echohawk and Bamaineo were in the school, all the seats in the back and near the wall were taken. They had to sit in the row right in front of Mr. Warner.

The schoolmaster glowered at his students, rapping a long thin cane across the top of his desk.

He shouted, and everybody groaned and punched his neighbor. Mr. Warner passed out pieces of paper and gave everyone a feather.

Mr. Warner cleared his throat and shouted again.

"What kind of bark is this, Echohawk? Each strip is the same." Bamaineo held up his piece of paper.

Mr. Warner looked right at Bamaineo and snarled like a bear. Then he cleared his throat again.

Echohawk and Bamaineo watched in bewilderment as the students dipped their feathers in bowls of what looked like black mourning paint. They all looked at Mr. Warner expectantly.

"Why are they dipping turkey feathers in mourning paint, Echohawk?" Bamaineo dipped his feather in the thick ink. A blob of it splashed on his paper.

As Mr. Warner spoke, the students scratched their feathers onto their pieces of paper.

"Echohawk, what are we supposed to be doing?" Bamaineo whispered loudly.

Echohawk put his hand to his lips and shook his head at his brother.

Mr. Warner cleared his throat and spoke again. A student next to Bamaineo dipped his feather into the ink and scratched across his paper. Bamaineo leaned over to get a better look.

"They are making signs," he exclaimed. "On the bark!"

"Little brother, shh—"

A clap of thunder seemed to come right out of Mr. Warner's mouth. The schoolmaster stood right in front of Bamaineo and snapped his cane across his desk, hitting Bamaineo's fingers.

Bamaineo put his smarting fingers in his mouth and shrank into his seat. Mr. Warner leaned down and thrust his face right into Bamaineo's face. Another clap of thunder roared out of Mr. Warner's mouth as his face turned red.

Mr. Warner marched back to his desk just as Bamaineo leaned over and threw up his morning corn on the floor.

Echohawk heard Mr. Warner groan over his ham, potatoes, and gravy. They were all back at the cabin for noon corn. The brothers sat silently at the table, their faces turned toward their plates. A teary-eyed Bamaineo nibbled at his food.

Echohawk was too stunned to eat. The morning had been awful. The English he had promised his father he would learn sounded like the snorts and snarls of animals as it burst from Mr. Warner's mouth. And why was he so angry all the time?

After Bamaineo threw up, Mr. Warner put them in a group of little children, and that was even worse. The little ones screeched like blue jays as they reached out to pull Echohawk's hair.

Mr. and Mrs. Warner talked back and forth, back and forth, Mr. Warner sounding angrier and angrier, until he left them with his wife in the cabin. Mrs. Warner smiled at them both, then turned her back as she cleared the table.

"What is the matter with you? Are you sick?" Echohawk whispered.

"No," Bamaineo whispered back.

"You are afraid? Of this man who does not even carry a weapon with him? Our father told us no one would hurt us. You must believe him. I do."

"Why was he shouting at me?"

Echohawk shrugged his shoulders. "You must not talk in front of him again."

"But why?"

"Jonathan, Bamaineo," Mrs. Warner said brightly.

"Now maybe they will send us home," Bamaineo said hopefully.

"No, little brother. We cannot go home until we learn

their language. Our father would be very angry if he knew we left, running like rabbits. We are Mohicans!"

With a great flourish, Mrs. Warner placed a kernel of corn on the table in front of them. She looked at them expectantly.

"One," she said.

By the time Mr. Warner came home for evening corn, Echohawk and Bamaineo were on their stomachs near the fire, tossing corn kernels in front of them and calling out the amounts in English.

Mrs. Warner scooped up the corn kernels and dumped them on the table in front of Mr. Warner.

She gestured for the brothers to stand next to him.

"Bamaineo," Mr. Warner said sternly. He seized Bamaineo's hand by the wrist. One by one, he picked up kernels and placed them in Bamaineo's hand. Bamaineo recited the numbers in a shaky voice.

"One, t-two, three, f-four—"

When Bamaineo had counted to ten, Mr. Warner nodded and transferred all the kernels into Echohawk's hand. One by one, he added ten more.

"Eleven, twelve, thirteen," Echohawk counted in a clear, confident voice. He looked the schoolmaster straight in the eye as he spoke. *"Twenty,"* he said triumphantly.

Mrs. Warner clapped her hands, then gave them little cakes with black walnuts inside.

"Cookies," she said.

The next morning Echohawk and Bamaineo were

counting again when they heard children shouting in the school yard. As Mrs. Warner shooed them out the door, the brothers saw students rushing out of the schoolhouse like bees out of a hive.

They stepped warily out into the school yard.

"Echohawk, look. The Abenaki are playing stick-ball."

As they ran toward the stickball court, two town boys stepped in front of them, blocking their way.

One boy drew a line in the dirt with his foot. He stood directly in front of Echohawk.

The town boys stood crouching with their feet wide apart, their hands folding and unfolding into fists, their jaws jutting out. They spoke back and forth, taunting the brothers with high-pitched voices that quavered around the edges.

There was something familiar about them. Even their faces—their glowing eyes, their sneering lips curled tightly around clenched teeth—reminded Echohawk of something.

Just like Gahko, he thought suddenly, *when he tries to hide his fear with anger. Why are they so afraid of me?*

One boy stepped forward until he was less than a hand's width away from Echohawk's face. The boy's eyes were coldly blue, gleaming like wet ice. As the town boy jeered at him, Echohawk studied his eyelashes in wonder. They were white and surrounded his blue eyes in long spikes.

"Snowflakes," Echohawk said. "Your eyelashes make me think of snowflakes."

The boy sniffed at Echohawk's clothes and made a face. He pulled at Echohawk's deerskin sleeve, then wiped his hand on his own shirt.

"They are afraid of me, Bamy," Echohawk said in a low voice. "And this one thinks our clothes are dirty and smell bad."

"Our mother did not make shirts that smell," Bamaineo said.

The other boy pushed Bamaineo so hard, he almost fell over. When Echohawk turned to help, the boy with the snowflake eyelashes grabbed Echohawk's long hair and pulled hard. As he pulled, he spoke in a girlish, squealing voice. The boy who'd pushed Bamaineo laughed. The boy with the snowflake eyelashes pulled harder.

Echohawk spun around and fixed on him his fierce hawk gaze. He narrowed his yellow-brown eyes into slits and waited for the boy to blink and look away. In an instant the boy was in the dirt and Echohawk was sitting on his chest, his knees pinning the boy's elbows to the ground. Echohawk glared at him in a sort of red haze of rage.

"I have had to fight all my life, and I have no fear of you," he shouted. "You will not stand in my face again, Chipmunk. You will not stand in the face of my brother, either."

The boy began to wail.

"I will not fight you here because of the shaman—"

99

Mr. Warner came up from behind and pulled Echohawk to his feet. He bellowed like a bear.

The boy scrambled upright and pointed a trembling finger at Echohawk's belt, where he kept his tomahawk. He wailed again, this time blubbering as well, because he was sobbing so hard.

Mr. Warner pointed to Echohawk's belt and held out his other hand.

Echohawk wouldn't even look at Mr. Warner as he pulled his tomahawk from his belt.

Mr. Warner turned to Bamaineo next and snarled. Bamaineo took a step back.

"Echohawk!"

"Give him your knife, Bamy. I will watch him carefully to see where he hides them," Echohawk said softly between clenched teeth.

Bamaineo gave up his knife.

The schoolmaster took hold of the brothers' deerskin shirts and marched them back to the cabin. Looking over his shoulder, Echohawk saw a half circle of boys watching him. The sobbing boy with the snowflake eyelashes kicked a clod of dirt in his direction.

After noon corn, Echohawk and Bamaineo were back in the school yard.

"Jonathan! Jonathan!" Another town boy ran over to them carrying three stickball rackets.

"Lacrosse? I don't know what you Indians call it."

The town boy held out two of the rackets. Echohawk nodded eagerly.

"This way!" Tossing the words back over his shoulders, the town boy ran toward the stickball court, and they followed him.

He handed them each a racket—a long, thin wooden pole of springy ashwood with a net made of grapevine at one end.

Echohawk studied the four Abenaki standing on the other side of the stickball court. They were tall; even the shortest was half a head taller than himself.

"Bamy, do you remember playing stickball against the Abenaki at the tribal meeting two summers ago?"

"Yes, I remember."

"They were so fast, but you were just as fast. And when you played between them, you were as slippery as a snake. No one could catch you, remember?"

"Yes," Bamaineo said. "I remember. I will play like that."

"Ian Miller." The town boy pointed at himself. "John House, Thomas Whitmore, James Appleby—"

"—Robert Shaw," the boy with the snowflake eyelashes said defiantly, his chin sticking straight out. He pointed to the boy who'd pushed Bamaineo and said, "William Croft."

Echohawk nodded to them all. He began pumping his arms up and down and back and forth to warm up his shoulders. The others did the same.

They all stood on their side of the center line; the Abenaki stood on their side of the line. It was a chilly day, but the Abenaki had their shirts off.

The team members nodded to the tallest Abenaki. He stared down at them and thrust out his chest to show off the panther tattoos on his arms and shoulders.

"Loxpa," Ian whispered to Echohawk.

Loxpa let out a great war whoop and tossed the ball straight into the air. As it fell, he scooped it up and ran toward the goal line. The Abenaki protected their side, tossing the ball from net to net. Bamaineo ran between them and caught the ball in his net. He turned abruptly and tossed the ball to Echohawk, who ran down the court and tossed it to Ian. Ian caught the ball in his net and ran down the rest of the court to the goal line.

One to zero, town team.

This time the town team got to toss the ball in the air.

Back and forth, back and forth, the teams played all recess. The Abenaki scored and scored again. Then Bamaineo slipped between them and tossed the ball to Echohawk, who could outrun anybody.

The score was tied when Mr. Warner called out from the doorway. The game abruptly stopped; everyone ran toward the school.

"Little brothers," Loxpa said softly behind them. The tallest Abenaki drew Echohawk and Bamaineo toward him. "I want to talk to you before going into the *school*."

"Explain, Loxpa," Echohawk replied in Abenaki.

"Explain?"

"Explain everything! Why is Mr. Warner so angry

with us? Why is the boy with the snowflake eyelashes even angrier? Yesterday morning we were with you and Mr. Warner in the *school.* Now we are with Mrs. Warner in her wigwam. Our father said much of what they want will make no sense. But nothing makes sense!"

"There is one rule to remember," Loxpa said. "You must never say anything in front of Joshua Warner if it is not in English."

"But we speak no English," Bamaineo said.

"Exactly. He will tolerate no Algonquin or Iroquois languages here. That means no Abenaki, Sokoki, Mohican. And no Mohawk."

"And what about those Mohawks?" Echohawk asked.

Loxpa shook his head. "We do not bother them. They do not bother us. We have enough trouble with Joshua Warner." He nodded to Bamaineo. "You play stickball very well. Your name is Bamaineo?"

"Yes. Thank you, Cousin."

"Perhaps tomorrow you would like to play on our team?" Loxpa asked. "When you run between us, you are like an eel slipping among the river rocks."

Bamaineo and Echohawk gazed up at Loxpa. He was almost twice the size of Bamaineo.

"Thank you, Cousin," Bamaineo said. "But I must play on my brother's team."

"I had heard about the white boy, Echohawk, living among the Mohicans. If you have any trouble—"

"I will have no trouble," Echohawk replied grimly.

"But thank you, Loxpa. What about the boy with the eyelashes like snowflakes?"

"The boy's name is Robert Shaw. About a year ago the French and Hurons swept down the river and attacked *Saratoga-on-the-Hudson*. They killed thirty people and took another one hundred captives back to the Canadas with them."

"So I have heard."

"You have?" Bamaineo exclaimed.

"The Hurons scalped everyone in his family except for Robert and his baby sister. They stole her."

"It still makes no sense for him to be angry with me," Echohawk protested. "We are not Huron."

"His anger is not at you, his anger is about you," Loxpa said thoughtfully. "He looks at you, Echohawk, and sees what his sister will become. He claimed you were trying to kill him."

"Kill him? That is why Mr. Warner took our weapons?"

Bamaineo said, "Cousin, where do you live? We are half a moon away from Abenaki land."

"Mrs. Warner is coming. She will teach both of you until you are ready to join the school. She did the same with me."

Mrs. Warner stood in front of them. "Jonathan, Bamaineo. *Hello*, Loxpa."

"Mrs. Warner," Loxpa said politely. He went into the school.

"Echohawk," Bamaineo said as they trotted after Mrs.

Warner, "you said those boys were afraid of you, not angry. Why are they afraid?"

"Nothing makes sense," Echohawk muttered.

"I am afraid of the Hurons," Bamaineo said softly. "And now we have no weapons."

"I have my musket, Bamy."

The Sky-Bears Moon gave way to the Moon of Fallen Leaves. The Moon of Fallen Leaves gave way to the Freezing Moon. By the Freezing Moon Echohawk and Bamaineo were almost ready to return to the school. They had been working very hard. They could count to one thousand in English, they could read the first-level schoolbooks, and they knew enough English to understand some of what people were saying, if those people spoke slowly.

The days shortened and turned cold. The leafless trees were no help against the winter wind that blew in from the Canadas. When the stickball court filled with snow, Echohawk, Bamaineo, Loxpa, Ian, and John built snow warriors and a *Fort Edward* snow fort. They threw snowball cannonballs at the French and Hurons, who'd come back to burn the town again, if only at recess.

When the river froze, they poured water on the toboggan runs so the runs froze. Screaming down the toboggan runs, the boys shot over the river as fast as hunted deer.

The nights were longer and bitterly cold. Echohawk unrolled their bearskin blankets for the winter. When they woke at dawntime, a light dusting of snow, blown in through the cracks in the log walls, had settled on everything. The bearskins, the attic floor, their hair, even their eyelashes were covered in snow.

One morning they woke to find Mr. Warner glaring at them.

"Just as I thought," Mr. Warner said. He flipped the bearskins off the bed and folded them under his arm. "What separates us from the savages, sir, is cloth," he said slowly. "It's time you learned it. No animal skins are used in this house."

Echohawk stood up. "Why?" he said in English.

"Why? Why?" Mr. Warner blinked at him in surprise. Echohawk glared into his eyes, but this time Mr. Warner glared right back.

"Because"—Mr. Warner scowled—"I said so."

The schoolmaster marched over to the landing and threw the bearskins down to the first floor. They landed with a thump, the claws *clack-clack*ing against the ladder on the way down.

Echohawk waited until Mr. Warner was on the first floor before creeping soundlessly to the ladder. He crouched down and watched the schoolmaster lock the bearskins into the far cupboard and place the key on the ledge above the front door.

Echohawk crept back to Bamaineo. "Glickihigan said to do everything the shaman says, but our father risked his life for those bearskins so we would not be cold in winter! I have seen where he has hidden them. I am taking them back."

He slammed his fists against the corn-husk mattress.

"Jonathan, Bamaineo," Mrs. Warner called to them. "Breakfast is ready."

"Yes," they shouted down to her.

"I am ready to face him," Echohawk said fiercely. "Even with no weapons I am ready."

Bamaineo held Echohawk's arm. "Do not show him your anger, or we will not only lose our weapons, we will lose our bearskins."

Echohawk's jaw dropped.

"We will ask Jerusha Warner to tell him she has given the bearskins away," Bamaineo said softly.

"What?"

"She will speak falsely for us. She does not like her husband much."

"You amaze me, little brother. How do you know these things?"

"Because I know."

CHAPTER TEN

THEY ATE THEIR MORNING CORN SILENTLY, Echohawk trying hard not to betray his anger with his face. He concentrated on stickball and hunting, Jerusha Warner's cooking, the turtle wigwam, and the Sugar Maple Moon. He tried to look cheerful and contented.

"When will these two be ready for school?" Mr. Warner demanded. He opened the front door.

"In a week or two, by Christmas, surely," Mrs. Warner answered back.

"Good-bye, Mr. Warner," the boys chanted together.

"See that they are, Jerusha." A blast of cold air and snowflakes blew in and pushed the fire sideways against the back of the chimney. The door slammed shut.

Echohawk gulped some tea to clear his throat.

"Jerusha Warner," he began, "we . . . need . . . our brother."

"I know you do, Jonathan. But your brother is here. I don't understand what you're saying."

"We need our brother, *Makwa* . . . bear."

Bamaineo pointed upstairs. "Cold. Night cold. Snow."

"Oh, dear." Mrs. Warner smoothed her blond hair back and rested her chin in her hands. "Couldn't you sleep by the fire?" She pointed to the fire and put her hands next to her face to gesture sleep.

They shook their heads and waited.

"No, he wouldn't like that, either." Mrs. Warner looked at them both. "All right, I'll think of something to tell Mr. Warner."

She dragged her chair over to the door and stood on it to reach for the key.

Echohawk leaned across the table. "Bamy, you were right."

Bamaineo smiled and ate another apple fritter.

Mrs. Warner opened the cupboard and the bearskins tumbled out. "Their weight," she groaned. "Where did you get them? Jonathan, where?"

"Glickihigan," Echohawk said as he scooped them up and ran up the ladder. He folded them in half carefully and hid them under the cornhusk mattress.

When you show your anger, your enemy has already won.

"Not this time, Father," Echohawk whispered to himself.

"Perhaps Mr. Warner wouldn't mind them so much if you took the claws out," she said to Bamaineo downstairs. She curled her fingers and held them in front of her. "Claws?"

From the ladder, Echohawk saw Bamaineo curl his fingers into claws too. He growled. Echohawk laughed and Mrs. Warner and Bamaineo joined in.

That evening Mrs. Warner served them steaming bowls of cornmeal cooked with milk, eggs, sugar, and butter.

"Instead of wooden bowls I thought we'd use my mother's china, Mr. Warner," she said nervously. "I know how you admire it."

Echohawk picked up his bowl and set it down quickly. The china bowl was much hotter than a wooden bowl would have been.

"Ow!" Bamaineo shouted. His bowl clattered to the uneven dirt floor. He blew on his palms to cool them.

Echohawk frowned at the cabin floor, at the pale yellow contents of the bowl spilling out onto the brown surface like a fan. The cornmeal steamed against the cold floor.

What does that remind me of?

Smoke, fire, screaming . . .

Echohawk sprang from the table and pressed his back against the cabin wall. His heart pounded; cold sweat poured from his palms. His muscles shook violently as though the snakes were back, racing and crawling under his skin.

"Jonathan, whatever is the matter?" Mrs. Warner asked.

Echohawk's chest heaved; he gasped for air.

Mrs. Warner stood in front of him. "Jonathan, I thought Indians liked all manner of corn dishes. You don't have to eat the corn pudding if you don't want it."

"C-corn p-pudding," he sputtered. Something about

steaming corn pudding spilling out onto brown creek water, spreading out like a fan. His knees gave way and he fell to the floor.

Mrs. Warner knelt on the floor in front of Echohawk. "Come back to the table, Jonathan," she said gently. "Give me your hand."

She waited patiently until Echohawk collected himself. He reached out a trembling hand. Mrs. Warner helped him to his feet.

Echohawk sat down quickly at the table, to ease his wobbly legs. They were all staring at him. Mrs. Warner and Bamaineo wore shock and concern on their faces. Mr. Warner frowned at him in surprise and impatience.

Echohawk put his face in his hands and waited for his gasping breath and pounding heart to return to normal.

Without being told to do so, the brothers did their homework in front of the fire every night. They went upstairs to bed exactly when Mrs. Warner told them to. They always said, "Good night, Mr. and Mrs. Warner," as they climbed the ladder for bed.

Then they would curl up under the cotton quilts and try to stay warm. Echohawk would wait until the Warners were asleep downstairs before unfolding the bearskins. In the dawntime he woke before everyone else and hid the bearskins under the corn-husk mattress.

More and more often the boys were sleepy in the afternoons, because they had to stay up so late. Mr. and Mrs. Warner would walk the floor underneath them, arguing and shouting at one another other far into the night.

The brothers would lie awake, hearing every word but understanding little of it:

"Mr. Warner, you cannot do this. I will not allow it."

"The lost lamb, Mrs. Warner. Why has God placed Jonathan in our household? So we may redeem him back to his own people."

"Jonathan has already lost one family. I will not be part of his removal from another."

"Jonathan *is* lost, Mrs. Warner, lost in a wilderness far beyond our ability to tolerate. But not, I believe, irretrievably so. When we move to Boston in May, he will accompany us."

"But Jonathan has a family. Mr. Glickihigan has put his trust in us—"

"If we decide—no, if I decide—to take Jonathan with us, you know and I know there is nothing Mr. Glickihigan can do about it."

"How can you even think that?"

"They are shouting about me again," Echohawk said softly.

His brother turned over and faced him. "How is it you have learned English so fast?"

"No, listen, little brother. They are shouting 'Jonathan' again and again—'Glickihigan' and 'Boston,' too."

"Mrs. Warner, I can scarcely imagine what that poor boy's life has been like, can you? Living in the forest with a pack of Indians? The brutality, the horror . . . It would be an act of kindness, of mercy, to bring Jonathan back to Boston with us. Let him see what the world is really like."

"His world is real enough."

"'The light shines in the darkness,' Jerusha. Let him finish his education at Harvard, as I did. Then return, and bring these wretched savages out of darkness. Surely you are as horrified as I am."

"In some respects I am. But you've got his whole life planned out for him."

"You've heard of captive exchanges, Jerusha. He's a captive. He's also just a boy living in the pure ignorance of savagery."

"You have given this a great deal of thought, Joshua. So have I. What about his brother?"

"Bamaineo? He goes back to his village with his father. They live ten, fifteen miles up the Hudson, as the crow flies. We can't save him, not yet. But we can save Jonathan."

"Those two are more than brothers—they live in each other's pockets! Poor Bamaineo would be bereft. They both would."

"They said my name," Bamaineo whispered. "What are they saying about us?"

"Our father is right. We must learn English as fast as possible. Wait here."

Echohawk waited until the Warners were shouting again before gently folding back the quilts. Soundlessly he got out of bed and crept to the ladder. He lay on his stomach and hung his head over the landing. Mr. Warner paced the floor, shouting while pounding his fist into the palm of the other hand. Mrs. Warner stood by the fireplace with her back straight and her chin out. But her hands were trembling and she kept her gaze on the table, where two cups of tea steamed.

"What are they fighting about, Echohawk?" Bamaineo whispered in his ear.

Echohawk jumped. "They will hear you, little brother."

Bamaineo thrust out his chin. "You did not hear me."

Echohawk pressed his mouth to his brother's ear. "We will wait until he is shouting again."

"Jerusha," Mr. Warner thundered from below. He pounded the tabletop so hard the teacups jumped.

"Now." They crept back to the bed while Mr. Warner shouted into the cold winter night.

"So?" Bamaineo asked. "Why are they arguing?"

"I wish I knew," Echohawk said uneasily. "They are arguing about me, and you, and our father. She is losing the argument."

"You've woken the boys," Echohawk heard Mrs. Warner scold from below. He sat up as she slowly climbed the ladder. Mrs. Warner's face was lit by a candle she held in one hand.

"Is there something wrong?" she asked.

"No. Good night, Mrs. Warner," Echohawk replied.

"Good night, Mrs. Warner." Bamaineo's voice sounded muffled against his pillow.

"Good night, then." She slowly stepped down the ladder.

"Maybe we are not learning English fast enough," Bamaineo whispered after she descended. "Maybe they think we are not smart enough."

"It is something else, little brother. Go to sleep."

"Maybe we eat too much food."

Echohawk laughed silently. "Maybe *you* eat too much food." He poked him in the stomach. "You are as fat as a woodchuck."

"I am not!" Then: "Echohawk?"

"Yes?"

"Maybe our deerskins make him angry the same way our bearskins do."

Echohawk considered for a moment. "No," he said finally. "Our clothes make him angry, but it's more than that. Go to sleep now."

Long after everyone else was sleeping, Echohawk lay awake. It was happening every night now: As soon as he closed his eyes, memories would try to push inside. Memories of kittens as silent as stones, of terrible nightmares, of corn pudding spreading out onto creek water like a fan, then fire in the woods, smoke, and screaming. Something about clean water . . .

And heart-stopping terror, purer and more horrible than he'd ever felt before. Or had he? The memories were like evil spirits, waiting to claim him.

"Go away," he whispered into the darkness. "I do not want to remember you."

CHAPTER ELEVEN

THEY WOKE TO THE SOUND OF rifles blasting in the woods.

Echohawk and Bamaineo rushed down the ladder in time to see Mr. Warner run out the front door holding his rifle.

"Turkeys! Turkeys!" he was shouting.

Mrs. Warner was still in her nightclothes. "Something of a tradition around here," she said, looking at their puzzled faces. "They all rush into the woods and shoot turkeys on Christmas morning. Sit down, I'll start breakfast. Merry Christmas to you both."

They took their usual seats at the table. On their plates were what looked like snow-white pairs of tiny fishing nets. Bamaineo turned his over and over on his plate.

"What are these, Echohawk?"

Mittens. The English word flew into Echohawk's mind. He slowly slipped his mittens onto his hands. *I know about these things,* he thought. *I have worn them before.* He turned his hands over and turned them back again, staring at the mittens.

He held up his shaking hands and looked at his brother. His heart started pounding.

Smoke, fire, screaming—

Again, the terror. Where does it come from?

"Like this, Bamaineo," he said, trying to keep his voice steady. "They are to warm your hands."

There is so much here in the white man's camp that reminds me of my first life. But I don't want to remember. Something terrible is at the end of it. He took a deep breath to calm himself.

"Bamaineo, look. Jonathan knows how to wear them." Mrs. Warner tugged the mittens over Bamaineo's hands. "There, see?"

"Thank you, Mrs. Warner," they said together.

Echohawk took off the mittens quickly as she scooped potatoes and ham into their bowls. She heaped a steaming pile of cinnamon-apple fritters onto the platter in front of them.

Loud footsteps echoed on the porch.

"Jerusha Warner! Jerusha Warner! Merry Christmas to you."

"Jonathan! Bamaineo! Merry Christmas!"

Jerusha opened the door. Two men and two boys hurried in, each holding a wild turkey. Cold air clung to them like a blanket.

"Mrs. Warner, we thought you would like two of these birds on your table today," one of the men said. The boys held up their turkeys proudly.

"Thank you so much, boys," Mrs. Warner replied,

accepting the turkeys. "John House and Ian Miller, isn't it? Merry Christmas to you both. You just missed Mr. Warner. Jonathan, Bamaineo, look who's here."

"We shot four turkeys," John said importantly as he sat down at the table. "His pa shot one, my pa shot two, and me."

"You?" Ian shouted. "You missed."

Ian and John stuffed hot apple fritters into their mouths.

"Jonathan, what are you going to do today?" John asked around a mouthful of fritter.

"School."

"School?" Ian and John hooted together.

"There's no school today," Ian explained. "It's Christmas."

"No school today?" Echohawk tried to catch Mrs. Warner's eye, but she was talking and laughing with Mr. House and Mr. Miller by the fire. "Bamaineo—"

"'You just missed Mr. Warner,'" Ian mimicked in a high, squeaky voice. "We wanted to miss old man Warner."

"We waited out in the woods for him to leave," John said. "My pa said he didn't want his Christmas ruined. Old man Warner'll be back, though. Look what he forgot." John pointed to a powder horn on the mantelpiece.

"What will you do, Ian? John?" Echohawk asked.

Ian made a face. "We've got a horde of girl cousins up from Albany. John's going to his grandpa's cabin out in the woods."

"I can now say I've met the famous Jonathan," one of the men said as he walked toward the table. "He's all my Ian talks about."

"Pa," Ian said in an exasperated voice.

"He's all John talks about, too," Mr. House added. "Now John wants wampum strings in his hair and turtle tattoos on his chest."

John ducked his head and reached for another apple fritter.

"What turtle tattoos?" Mr. Warner shouted from the door.

Mr. Warner stomped across the room to the table. He seized Echohawk by the arm and lifted him to his feet.

"Turtle tattoos?" Mr. Warner repeated in a cold, hard voice. "What does he mean, turtle tattoos?"

Echohawk gasped, too panicked to comprehend. Mr. Warner's face was as red as war paint, his angry syllables no more intelligible than a Mohawk's.

"Jonathan, Mr. Warner wants to see your turtles," Ian whispered slowly, tapping his own chest.

"Yes?" Echohawk opened his shirt. Three six-pointed turtles lay neatly tattooed across his white skin.

Do you see? Only a Turtle clan warrior who has had a Vision Quest can wear the turtles. They are a mark of honor.

But Mr. Warner stared at his turtles in horror. "Savagery," he hissed through his teeth. "Darkness."

Echohawk looked back at Mr. Warner with the proud, cold gaze of a hawk.

"I never, *never* want to see those savage marks again,"

Mr. Warner said in a slow, hard voice. "Close your shirt."

Echohawk narrowed his eyes into slits. He slowly pulled his shirt closed. "They not for you, Mr. Warner."

"We were just leaving," Mr. House announced as the Houses and Millers edged toward the door.

"Merry Christmas," Mrs. Warner said weakly.

Echohawk heard a "Good-bye, Jonathan" as the front door slammed shut.

"Jerusha," Mr. Warner roared, "you're not even dressed!"

Echohawk said quietly, "My father never speak to my mother that way."

"Sit down!"

"Jonathan, Bamaineo," Mrs. Warner said briskly. "Finish your breakfasts and put your winter wraps on. We've got turkeys to pluck before Luke Warner and his family arrive."

Later that morning Echohawk and Bamaineo were on the back porch wearing their wolfskin robes and plucking the wild turkeys. They were supposed to be stuffing the feathers into a sack to save for pillows, but the wind was blowing so hard that the downy feathers were blowing right out of their hands.

Then it started to snow. Great, fat snowflakes whirled around them, looking just like the downy turkey feathers.

"I have the feather, I have it!" Bamaineo shouted as he charged off the porch.

"That is not a feather—that is a snowflake," Echohawk shouted. "Your eyes are as weak as an old woman's."

Bamaineo reached up with his mittened hand. "Got it!" He ran back to the porch and shoved his hand under Echohawk's nose. "See?"

But when he opened his hand, it was empty. "See, Bamy?" Echohawk teased. "That was a snowflake."

"Another feather!"

Bamaineo jumped off the porch and dove into a snowdrift. "Echohawk! This is not a snowflake, this is not a feather, this is a *Christmas* snowball."

Echohawk looked up just in time to get a snowball in his face.

He jumped off the porch and pushed Bamaineo into the deepest snowdrift. They were rolling around in the snow, laughing and whirling each other into the drifts, when Jerusha Warner opened the back door.

"Boys! Boys! My turkeys! What have you done with my turkeys?"

JING, jing, JING, jing, JING, jing, JING, jing . . .

"They're here," she shouted. "Luke Warner!" She motioned with her arm for the boys to come around the far side of the cabin.

They ran around to the front in time to see a well-dressed man, a woman, and two small children get out of a horse-drawn sleigh. The horse was wearing a collar of sleigh bells around its shoulders. The sleigh was painted bright green with red runners.

121

"Luke, Elizabeth, Samuel, Rebecca, merry Christmas!" called Mrs. Warner.

"Merry Christmas, Joshua, merry Christmas, Jerusha," Luke Warner said. "Who are these two?" He pointed at Echohawk and Bamaineo.

"They are staying with us for the school year," Jerusha explained. "All the Indian schoolchildren stay with local families. This is Jonathan; this is Bamaineo."

"Hello," Luke Warner said, shaking hands with each one.

"Hello, Luke Warner," Echohawk said. *I remember those eyes. The color of woodsmoke in sunshine.*

"Oh, yes. I remember you," Luke Warner replied. "You traded a bearskin for a musket and some cooking pots. Merry Christmas."

"Mama," Rebecca exclaimed, "those boys have wolf heads on their heads. Look."

"Goodness, what have they been doing?" Elizabeth Warner asked.

"They're supposed to be plucking turkeys." Jerusha laughed.

"Turkeys! They don't want to pluck turkeys on Christmas. Where are these turkeys? I'll help you, Jerusha. Samuel, Rebecca, stay with your father."

"Bamaineo," Echohawk said excitedly. "We no longer have to pluck the turkeys. I understood what they were saying!"

Samuel and Rebecca stopped laughing and throwing

snowballs as their uncle slammed the front door. Joshua Warner shivered and glared at the winter sky.

Luke winked at the boys. "Is my brother always this cheerful, or is it just because it's Christmas?" he called out.

"Luke," Mr. Warner said. "You need some help, I suppose?"

Echohawk and Bamaineo stood back as the men led the stomping, jittery horse into the barn. Echohawk watched, fascinated. The horse had steam coming out of its nose and more steam rolling off its back and chest.

Bamaineo studied the smooth imprints the sleigh blades left in the snow. He traced the horse's hoofprints with his finger.

"Echohawk, a *horse* would be easy to track. I wonder if they taste like deer."

Echohawk laughed. "You must be hungry, little brother."

In the cabin Jerusha and Elizabeth passed around bowls of corn pudding and slices of smoked ham.

"I'll say grace," Mr. Warner announced. Echohawk saw Mrs. Warner's mouth drop open as she bowed her head.

What is he doing now? Echohawk thought as Mr. Warner bowed his head and began to speak. He spoke for a long time.

"Echohawk," Bamaineo mouthed silently, "why is he talking to his food?"

123

Echohawk covered his mouth and shook his head.

"Don't eat too much," Jerusha said gaily after the amens. "We're having a big Christmas dinner later."

Luke said, "Jonathan, Bamaineo, perhaps you'd like a sleigh ride after our noon meal? I'll bet my brother has never taken you anywhere for sport."

"When you have forty students entrusted to you, we'll see how much free time you have for sport," Mr. Warner retorted.

"Joshua, it's Christmas," Mrs. Warner said in a warning voice.

After noon corn, Luke Warner stepped to the side door that led to the barn. "Jonathan, Bamaineo, how about that sleigh ride?" He held his hands together as though holding the reins, stomped his foot, and whinnied. "Joshua, would you hold Tim's head while we get in? I'll unhitch him when we return."

They put on their winter robes again. Reverend Warner led Tim out of the barn. Luke Warner stepped into the sleigh and sat down in the driver's box.

"Hold him steady. All right, boys, step in. This is Tim."

Tim turned his head all the way around to see who was sitting in the sleigh.

"Easy, Tim. Thank you, Joshua," Luke Warner said. "Ready, Jonathan? Ready, Bamaineo?"

The brothers were sitting on either side of him, gripping the sides of the sleigh tightly and trying not to look scared.

"Hello, brother," Bamaineo whispered to Tim.

"Tim! Walk on!" Luke Warner touched Tim's right shoulder with a long whip. Tim immediately began to walk.

"Tim! Trot on!"

Tim began to trot.

"We won't be long," Luke shouted behind him as Mr. Warner went back into the cabin.

JING, jing, JING, jing, JING, jing, JING, jing, the sleigh bells rang out in the crisp winter air.

"Tim, *hyah!*" Luke shouted. Tim broke into a faster trot.

"Bamaineo, take these reins for a minute. Hold them tightly, but not too tightly." Luke Warner gave a wide-eyed Bamaineo the reins while he rummaged around in the backseat.

"You boys put this around you; we're going to be cold in a minute." Luke shook out a bearskin and tucked it around their waists.

"You like our brother!" Bamaineo gasped in English.

"Of course I like Jonathan. I like you, too, Bamaineo. You can give me the reins again. Thank you."

Echohawk said, "Luke Warner, you like our brother the bear."

"You have a brother who's a bear," Luke said slowly. His eyes twinkled. "Why isn't he in school?"

"No." Bamaineo laughed and held up a corner of the bearskin. "You have—you like."

"Do I like your brother the bearskin? Now I understand. Yes, it's cold outside."

125

They thought about this for a while.

"We thought . . . white men don't like . . . our brother the bear," Echohawk explained.

"*My* brother, you mean. My brother doesn't like much of anything. I'm not my brother, Jonathan. Tim! *Gyup!*"

Tim broke into a canter. The wind whistled through Echohawk's ears as the sleigh seemed to fly over the snow. *This is the way a hawk must feel,* he thought, *gliding through the air.*

But it *was* cold. They burrowed under the bearskin and leaned closer to Luke Warner.

In a few minutes they were in the town. Luke pulled Tim up into an easy trot around the square. The cabins, stores, and church were closed up tight against the cold. Smoke rose from the chimneys and wreathed the trees behind the town in gray.

"The stone wigwam," Bamaineo shouted. "Look!"

"That is where I saw the tiny panther, little brother." *Where the memories began.*

Bamaineo studied the stone tavern walls. "If we knew enough English, we could ask Mr. Warner's brother why the stones have agreed to stand on one another."

Instead of turning toward home, Luke Warner turned right at the end of the square, and they traveled south for a while on the river road.

They passed the ruins of a grand, beautiful home. Luke nodded to the blackened walls and collapsed roof.

"French? Huron?" Echohawk asked.

"Yes. The Schuyler home. The old Dutch patroon family. They haven't yet rebuilt after the attack."

Farther south, Echohawk saw cabin windows deep in the woods. In the solid blue twilight, the windows were lit up orange from the firelight within. Farther away there were more cabins. They passed another little town.

So many people, Echohawk thought. *Where do they all come from? How far will Glickihigan have to travel next winter for fur, and the winter after that?* He felt colder, but no bearskin could warm him. The cold was inside.

"Bamy," he called out, "I have been thinking about our father. I hope he is living and among our brothers the Delaware."

No answer.

"Bamy?" Echohawk leaned sideways. His brother lay bundled in the bearskin, his head in Luke Warner's lap.

"I think your brother's asleep, Jonathan. He hasn't moved since we left Saratoga-on-the-Hudson."

After Christmas dinner Echohawk, Bamaineo, Samuel, and Rebecca lay in front of the fire. Bamaineo brought out a winter game he'd brought from home called pick-up sticks.

"See us. Watch," Echohawk said to Rebecca and Samuel.

Bamaineo shook the tall wooden box, opened it, and tossed the sticks into a pile. He began picking up the smooth, polished sticks one at a time, careful not to move any of the others while doing so. As he picked up the third stick, another moved.

"You are out of practice, Bamy," Echohawk said in a low voice so Mr. Warner couldn't hear him. "I am next."

Echohawk began to play, but as soon as he picked up one stick, another fell off the pile.

"Who is out of practice?" Bamaineo whispered back.

"My turn! My turn!" Rebecca shouted. "I know how to play now."

From out of the corner of his eye, Echohawk saw Luke and Joshua Warner standing by the front door, smoking pipes. The cold outside air pulled the smoke through the cracks between the logs. Mr. Warner scowled at Luke.

"Brother," Joshua said sternly, "you knew this boy was living with the savages and did nothing?"

This boy, Echohawk thought to himself. *The shaman is talking about me again.* He tried to listen closely.

"I've known Glickihigan for years," Luke replied. "We're business partners. The two of them brought in a magnificent bearskin last September. Didn't you, Jonathan?" Luke called out. "A bearskin?"

Echohawk grinned. "Our brother," he answered back. "There, you see, Joshua?"

"You did nothing to help this boy?"

"My guess is Jonathan's lucky to be alive."

"He is coming with us"—the schoolmaster had raised his voice slightly—"back to Boston in May."

"Does Glickihigan know this?" Luke asked.

He is . . . coming . . . with us. Echohawk repeated the words in his mind. *Back to Boston in May.* He frowned. *Glickihigan? Why would our father go to Boston in May?* He glanced at Luke and Joshua Warner. They were both looking right at him. Quickly, Echohawk looked down at the pick-up-sticks game. *He means me!* May . . . *the Dogwood Moon or the Fish Running Moon.*

Echohawk watched them out of the corner of his eye until he was sure they were no longer looking at him.

"Bamy," he said in a low, trembling voice, "I know now what it is Mr. Warner and his wife shout about at night."

"When they speak of *Jonathan?*"

"Yes. They are leaving this camp, at the Dogwood Moon. He wants to take me with him!"

Samuel Warner punched Echohawk on the arm. "It's your turn."

Bamaineo shrugged his shoulders. "Our father will return before then. We will be home long before the Dogwood Moon."

"And if he does not return? If Glickihigan has been captured by the Iroquois? What will we do then, little brother?"

Bamaineo, shocked, looked into Echohawk's face.

Samuel punched him on the arm again. "If you don't want your turn, can I have it?"

"No, me!" Rebecca shouted. "Let me."

"Yes. Girl." Echohawk motioned to the sticks.

"No fair," Samuel shouted. "I asked first."

"Ladies first," Rebecca said.

Echohawk felt cold even though he was closest to the fire. He couldn't stop shivering.

My Vision Quest—the hawk flies alone.

"What will we do? Bamy, what will we do?"

"It is easy. Our father said he will come for us two suns before the Sugar Maple Moon. He will be walking downriver, and we will be walking upriver. We will meet him on the riverbank and be home in time for the Maple Sugar Festival."

"The Iroquois torture their captives to death."

"Our father is not dead!"

"Shh. If the worst has happened, Nehjao of the Wolf clan will say yes for me to stay, but Makwa and Gahko will say no."

"Gahko is a boy—he has no say," Bamaineo answered.

"By the Sugar Maple Moon he will be older than thirteen winters. He will be a man, like me. He will have a say. And Mr. Warner knows where we live. He will come for me."

Bamaineo gazed into the fire, thinking.

"Then Tanebao Sachem will stop Gahko," Bamaineo said. "Then our sachem will kill Mr. Warner for you and throw him into the *Hudson* . . . I mean, the Muhekunetuk."

Our sachem is an old man, Echohawk thought. *What can he do?*

"Tanebao Sachem can do only what the clans want. If the worst has happened, I can never go back to the turtle wigwam." Echohawk's voice was shaking. "I can never go back. What are we going to do?"

"I win!" Rebecca shouted at Echohawk. "I win!"

"That's because you cheated," Samuel said.

That night, after Luke Warner took his family home in the sleigh, Echohawk lay awake and thought about the Sugar Maple Moon.

The first night the Sugar Maple Moon rose in the sky was the first sign of spring. It was also the best night of the year. The sap was poured into a huge basket made from tightly woven grass. The sap boiled all night over hot stones while the clans sang and danced or told stories far into the dawntime. When the syrup was finally ready, Makwasi would ladle spoonfuls onto clean snowballs and everyone could have as much maple sugar snow as he wanted. There would always be a snowball fight or two by morning corn.

"There is no place for me to go," Echohawk whispered. "Without Glickihigan, there is no place for me to live."

"Our father is not dead," Bamaineo repeated fiercely. "But if he does not return, we will start our own camp, to the west, brother. We will live on our own."

THE DAY AFTER CHRISTMAS was a Sunday. Echohawk, Bamaineo, and the Warners sat down to morning corn: bacon and eggs, fried apples, tea, and corn bread with butter.

"Mr. Warner," Mrs. Warner said, "yesterday Jonathan offered to shoot wild turkeys. Perhaps we should take him up on his offer."

Echohawk looked up eagerly. "Turkeys. You . . . need turkeys?"

"Your students' parents have been very generous with smoked venison and pork," Mrs. Warner went on. "But those fresh turkeys were so good yesterday. Wouldn't it be nice to have fresh meat? Smoked meat is so salty. I think Jonathan would enjoy it, too."

Echohawk watched as Mr. Warner slowly buttered a piece of corn bread. "If you want to, Jonathan," Mr. Warner replied. "But it is my opinion that you and your brother should spend the day with your books. I must prepare for church."

Mr. Warner pushed his plate away and left the table.

"Jonathan . . . *naahmao* . . . yes, please," Mrs. Warner said. "We do need *naahmao*. Isn't that what you call them? Wild turkeys?"

Echohawk sprang from the table and rushed up the ladder. He came down a few moments later with Thunderpath and his wolfskin winter robe and hood.

"*Nokekik*," he said. "We need . . . corn." He made a crushing motion with his hands.

"Turkey bait." Mrs. Warner laughed. "I see."

The storeroom next to the fireplace was filled with apples, smoked and dried venison, even smoked chickens. Sides of pork and ham lay in tubs of salt brine. A basket of eggs and bags of vegetables stood next to the wall nearest the fireplace. The wall was just cool enough: the eggs and vegetables would stay cold but not freeze.

Mrs. Warner opened a bag filled with crushed dried corn. Echohawk stuffed handfuls of the cracked corn into his waist pouch, then ran out the front door to look at the weather. Bamaineo followed at his heels.

"Echohawk, can I go?" his brother asked.

"No, little brother, you will stay here. Naahmao are clever, and this is not a good hunt day." Echohawk frowned at the swirling snow. "It is too windy, and the snow is too dry. Their tracks have disappeared already. I should have left in the dawntime."

"But I want to go!"

"No. You did not even bring your bow and arrows with you."

"I will ask for my knife back. Then we can go."

"You are not thinking, Bamy. I know where Mr. Warner has hidden our weapons. If we ask for them back, he may hide them someplace else. You talk too much, you ask too many questions. Go inside. I need to think today."

"Think about what, Echohawk?"

"Go inside." Echohawk pushed his brother back into the cabin and slammed the door. "And I will know if you are following me."

As he put on his snowshoes, Echohawk could hear Bamaineo kicking the door. "I am a good hunter! I am!" he was shouting. "I do not talk too much!"

Kick, kick.

"Echohawk, I am a good hunter. Echohawk!"

Kick, kick.

How good it felt to be alone in deep woods again! It was so quiet. His snowshoes made light, swishing sounds as he walked farther and farther away from the cabin and the school. The air was sweet and cold. The wind caught snowflakes drifting lightly through the forest and blew them against his face.

I will head downhill and search a creekbed for tracks.

He stopped. *No: The creek water is frozen; the turkeys will eat snow when they are thirsty. There will be no tracks near water.*

Echohawk took off his new mittens and spit into his hands. He rubbed the spit on his cheeks, then turned around slowly, checking for wind direction. Wind from the west blew against his face and chilled it.

From the west—that meant the trees might still have tracks underneath them on the east side. The cold air had a touch of sweet pine in it. He drank in the air like cold cider.

Echohawk headed north for a long time, checking the east sides of oaks, maples, pines, ash, and beeches with low-lying branches. The branches had to be low because turkeys slept in trees at night, and they were too heavy to fly upward very far.

There! On the east side of a tamarack whose branches swept the ground—three prongs in front, one in back— turkey tracks.

Echohawk sprinkled cracked corn around the tree. He took off his wolfskin robe, spread it on the ground, and settled into the snow to wait. The sun was dropping slowly out of the gray winter sky. The wind died down, and there was no sound except for his own breathing.

They would be coming back to roost soon.

Alone with his thoughts, without English to learn, without Mr. Warner to avoid, without Bamaineo asking more questions than stars in the night sky, Echohawk let his mind drift.

He wondered when he had last been alone. Really alone. Back at camp he'd hide in a tree, bowstring taut and arrow ready, and wait for small animals to come out of their burrows.

But that was before the Warners, before Thunderpath,

before our mother died. Waiting in trees! The great hunter!

Echohawk smiled to himself. That was so long ago.

What am I doing here? What am I doing here? This is not even a good sun for hunting—but there will be no hunting tomorrow, because tomorrow is a sun for school. Glickihigan said we will not understand much of what they want, and here I am, not understanding.

Why am I learning a language I will never use, learning about people I will never see again?

And why did Glickihigan send us here? We should be with him, trapping in the Ohio country.

Our father said I may feel a pull toward them. Do I?

He let his mind go blank and waited for the answer to come, like a river turtle bobbing slowly to the surface.

Maybe.

He caught his breath and thought about all the things he liked—stickball, the sleigh and Tim, the food, mittens, candles, snow forts and toboggans, Mrs. Warner, John and Ian, and sharing the corn-husk mattress every night with Bamaineo.

But there is so much here I don't like, too. Mr. Warner, and sitting in a cabin for an entire sun learning to read. That is not the same as staying motionless for half a morning while hunting.

Bamaineo likes and dislikes the same things, so we are the same. This is not our home.

Echohawk shook his head. He knew in his heart that he and his brother were not the same. He felt painfully separate, as though the Turtle clan were caught up in a swift current and he, left behind on the riverbank, could only watch them drift away from him.

The hawk hunts and lives alone.

I am learning English so much faster than Bamy. It is as though I am not learning it but . . . remembering it, remembering so many things like mittens, horses, and eating food set down on a table. I remember Christmas, *too—the excitement, presents, and good things to eat.*

Where are these memories coming from? Why do they make me so terrified? Shadows, smoke, and darkness lit slowly by the sun.

Echohawk's eyes widened. *Glickihigan sent me here to learn about these shadows and the pull I feel toward them, to decide which way to walk.*

A noise. Echohawk kept his body still and turned his head slowly in the direction of the noise.

A *bamain*—a great male elk—stepped through the trees, cautiously sniffing the air, stopping to listen at every footstep.

The salt from the smoked venison, Echohawk thought. *My turkey bait smells salty like the storeroom, like smoked meat.*

The elk was huge and had a white ruff like a fur collar around his broad shoulders. Powerful neck muscles held his proud head tall. *His antlers are growing back already,* Echohawk thought with a grin. *By the Strawberry Moon, they will be bigger than Bamaineo.*

Bamaineo! He was supposed to be here. His spirit-brother has come out of the forest to see him!

The *bamain* and Echohawk stared at each other. The

137

elk and his brother had the same soft, questioning brown eyes.

"Bamain Sachem," Echohawk said softly, "I told your little brother to stay at the cabin today because he did not bring his bow and arrows to the English camp. I did not know you were looking for him. I am sorry. I will be taking him home soon; I will not leave him alone. Do not worry: He is my little brother too."

The *bamain* stared at Echohawk and seemed to hesitate, to nod in his direction, before bounding into the forest again.

"Thank you for coming, Bamain Sachem, but I already know which way to walk."

"Little brother, I saw your spirit-brother today," Echohawk whispered that night in the attic.

Bamaineo sat up in the bed. There was just enough moonlight for Echohawk to see his startled face.

"What did he look like?"

"He was huge. Beautiful. His antlers will be bigger than you this summer. He was looking for you. And me."

"I have never seen him," Bamaineo said bitterly. "I could have seen him today. Was he bounding?"

"He was running and jumping away, yes. You will see him. I told him we would be going home soon, that he should look for you in camp."

Bamaineo lay down again and put his head on Echohawk's shoulder. "I could have seen him today," he repeated.

"You will."

"You shot no naahmao, Echohawk."

"No, I left them eating the nokekik, Bamy. Your spirit-brother came to see me in that place. I could never shoot them there."

Bamaineo sat up again. "Never call me Bamy again, now that my spirit-brother has tried to see me. My name is Bamaineo, the Bounding Elk."

Echohawk smiled up at him. "You are right. Never again, Bamaineo."

THE FREEZING MOON gave way to the Moon of Great Cold, and the Moon of Great Cold gave way to the Moon of Deep Snow. As the winter deepened, and the snow piled up higher than a man's head, school stopped altogether for weeks at a time. The Reverend Warner would ring the school bell hard when he thought the snow was packed down enough for the students to walk on. The church in town rang its bell in answer to the school bell. One by one, students would trudge through the forest trails and follow the snow paths in the school yard to the school.

Living with the schoolmaster, Echohawk and Bamaineo had no time off for snow days, regardless of the weather outside. They worked hard at their English, knowing how pleased Glickihigan would be, and knowing that the Sugar Maple Moon was the next moon.

In the last half of the Moon of Deep Snow, the snow lost its feather lightness as the bitter cold finally broke. As the days grew milder, the snow became heavy and wet. The earth around the creeks and along the sides of the cabin and school turned to mud as icicles dripped all the way to the ground. But the nights were still cold, and in the evening when the sun went down, the snow had a hard crust on it.

On a clear night, Echohawk left the cabin and walked toward the school yard. The walls of the snow paths came up over his head, and his moccasined feet had to punch through thick crusts of ice. The sound of crunching footsteps was the only sound in the silent darkness.

He shivered in his wolfskin robe as he waited for the moon to rise. Wind from the river whispered through the pines and rocked them back and forth in the starshine. The bits of ice on the snow sparkled like the stars. When the three-quarters moon rose, it drifted upward like a wide, curled feather floating in the night wind.

He studied the moon carefully. They could leave in five suns.

"Seven suns to the Sugar Maple Moon," he said softly to Bamaineo in the attic that night.

"We will leave in five suns. We must get ready," Bamaineo whispered back. He sighed happily. "Soon we will see our father; soon we will be sleeping in the turtle wigwam again. We will be eating maple sugar again."

"Last year you ate so much maple sugar snow, you threw up, remember?"

"I threw up because I ate too much snow. I was too cold inside."

"That was not the reason, Bamaineo."

Piece by piece over the next few days, they hid their extra winter clothes and moccasins in the forest by the river. On the second night, when Mr. and Mrs. Warner were sound asleep, Echohawk crept downstairs silently. He took their tomahawks and knives from where the schoolmaster had hidden them behind the cords of firewood. Echohawk rolled each one separately in his deerskin shirt so they would not rattle as he took them up the ladder. These they hid with their extra winter clothes by the river. The last to be hidden were their bearskins and snowshoes.

"Echohawk," his brother said softly on the third night. "I want to give Jerusha Warner a present. To say good-bye."

"No! She will tell her husband we are leaving."

Bamaineo flipped over on his stomach. "But she did not tell him about the bearskins."

"This is different." He put his hand on his brother's neck. "He will look in her face and know something has changed. Promise me you will not tell her."

"If we left a present for her, on the night we leave, she would be as surprised as he."

"Bamaineo, you cannot let your face show anything!"

"I have thought of a good present. I will lay it on her sleeping platform when we leave. I want to give her a present," he said stubbornly. "And you cannot let your face show anything, either."

The next morning Echohawk and Bamaineo watched Mr. Warner to see if he would ring the school bell. But the school bell sat on the mantelpiece all through morning corn. The brothers looked at one another and sighed—another snow day.

After Mrs. Warner cleared the dishes, Mr. Warner sat down with them to supervise their lessons.

"Bamaineo," he said, "sit by the fire and practice writing your alphabet. I'll ask you to recite later.

"Jonathan," he continued briskly, "we'll read from William Bradford, *Of Plymouth Plantation*, about the first people to come to the Massachusetts Bay Colony and their first day. The Pilgrims. Begin." He pointed to a passage.

Echohawk picked up the book and began to read aloud. He read slowly, haltingly, like a newborn fawn just learning to walk. Mr. Warner helped him with words he couldn't read.

"'Afterward they directed their course to come to the other shore, for they knew it was a neck of land they were to cross over, and so at length got to the seaside . . . and by way found a pond of clear, fresh water, and shortly after a good quantity of clear ground where the Indians had set corn . . . and heaps of sand newly paddled with their hands. Which, digging up, found in them divers fair Indian baskets filled with corn. So, their time limited, they returned to the ship lest they should be in fear of their safety; and took with them the corn.'"

"Very good," Mr. Warner said. "And what did you learn?"

Echohawk took a deep breath. "Mr. Warner, they took corn from the Wampanoag."

Mr. Warner's face darkened. "What did you say?"

"If hungry, it is all right to take, but must . . . give back. They did not give back to the Wampanoag people."

Mr. Warner snatched the book from Echohawk's hands. "I'm sure they gave something back," he said as he scanned the page.

"The book does not say. Now Wampanoag is . . . are . . . almost gone. There is . . . no place in Massachusetts for them to live."

Mr. Warner snapped the book closed. "You're learning English very rapidly, Jonathan."

"No," Echohawk said quickly. "I'm not learning your English."

"It's your English, too, Jonathan. Surely you don't intend to be a filthy savage your whole life."

"No," Echohawk said softly. Anger stirred inside him, like a fire springing to life.

"Are you saying English is *not* yours, Jonathan?"

"No," he said, watching Bamaineo by the fire.

When you show your anger . . .

"So English is yours? Which is it, boy?"

Echohawk took a deep breath and looked right into the schoolmaster's face. His own face was as calm and smooth as the pool above the waterfall.

"English . . . good," he said softly. He smiled.

144

"Excellent. You're making excellent progress, Jonathan."

At noon recess on the last day, the brothers and their
friends wandered to the farthest edge of the school yard.
Echohawk stood facing the schoolhouse door, to keep
an eye on Mr. Warner's comings and goings.

"Tell old man Warner to pound salt," Ian Miller said.

"Ian's right, Jonathan," John House said. "He can't tell
you what to do or where to live."

"You don't know," Echohawk said. "Our mother . . .
is dead. Maybe our father, too. Mr. Warner . . . can do
anything."

"He doesn't want Bamaineo?" Ian asked.

Echohawk shook his head.

"Why do you think your father's dead?" John asked.

Echohawk sighed. The Algonquin and Iroquois people were enemies. Had always been enemies. Always
like two panthers who meet in the forest. How could he
begin to explain?

"Where will you go?" Ian asked.

"West."

"Iroquois lands." John whistled softly. "Dangerous."

"Your name isn't really Jonathan, is it?" Ian asked.
"That's not what Bamaineo calls you."

"No."

"So where did 'Jonathan' come from?" Ian asked.

"I don't know where Jonathan comes from. He is a
boy . . . he is a name . . . he is not me."

"Don't you ever wonder?"

145

"Wonder?"

"Think about . . . who you are?"

Echohawk frowned. "I know . . . who I am, Ian."

Nobody said anything for a moment.

"We decided to give you this," Ian said. "If you're going west, you'll need it." Ian handed Echohawk a strip of cloth, tightly wound, about an inch and a half wide.

"Cut off pieces and wrap your lead in them, to load your rifle," Ian explained. "My father says cloth is much better than deerskin for wrapping lead. It's lighter and catches the spark better. If old man Warner were after me, I'd head west too."

"Yes, Ian and John. Better than deerskin. Thank you." Echohawk tucked the cloth into his waist pouch. "I say good-bye to Loxpa."

The tallest Abenaki squatted on his heels at the farthest edge of the school yard to talk to Bamaineo and Echohawk.

Loxpa greeted them softly. "Cousins."

"Loxpa!" Bamaineo shouted in delight.

"We hear you are leaving."

"Yes. Before the Sugar Maple Moon. The shaman wants my brother with him in *Boston.*"

"Do not call him a shaman, Cousin. He is no holy man. Your brother does not want to go with him to *Boston.*"

"No. Of course not, Loxpa."

"Next comes the Earth Drying Moon and we will be playing stickball again. I enjoyed our games together."

"We must go, Loxpa. I will miss you and our stickball games."

"You are afraid of him. You and Echohawk are afraid of Joshua Warner."

Bamaineo stirred uneasily. "Echohawk is not afraid of anything." He kicked at a stone with his foot.

Loxpa and Echohawk exchanged glances and smiled. "Bamaineo," Loxpa said, "Joshua Warner is afraid of *you*. He is terrified of us."

"The sha— Joshua Warner is afraid of me?"

"How is it that our people have lived here for so long and so well without him? This is what terrifies him. And Echohawk." Loxpa threw back his head and laughed. "Should Joshua Warner wake up screaming in the night, it is because he was dreaming of Echohawk."

"Echohawk?" Bamaineo asked.

"He wants us to become like him, and here is one of his who has become like us," Loxpa explained.

"I'm not one of his!" Echohawk replied indignantly.

"Exactly. Here."

Loxpa reached into his waist pouch and tossed Bamaineo a brand-new stickball. It was stuffed with deer hair and wrapped tightly with thin strips of deerhide.

Bamaineo tossed the ball into the air. "Thank you, Loxpa. I will think about what you have said to me."

"Perhaps we will see you again, Loxpa," Echohawk said.

"Perhaps. But your people are moving west and the Abenaki are moving north. This is my last year in *Saratoga-on-the-Hudson*."

"This is good-bye, then," Bamaineo said sadly.

Loxpa nodded. "Good-bye."

That night, Echohawk and Bamaineo sat down to their last meal together with the Warners. The brothers had already agreed to eat as much as they could; who knew when they would eat again?

"Bamaineo, more corn pudding and ham?"

"Thank you, Mrs. Warner."

"Jonathan?"

"Thank you, Mrs. Warner."

Mrs. Warner gave them each another scoop of corn pudding and a slice of ham.

"Well," she said. "Everyone is so hungry tonight."

"Yes, isn't this delightful?" Mr. Warner said. "We are having our dinner with two young gentlemen this evening."

A piled-high plate of black-walnut cookies was waiting right in front of him. Echohawk had never tasted anything so delicious as those black-walnut cookies. Nothing was better on a cold winter night in front of the fire than eating black-walnut cookies and drinking hot sassafras tea.

Mrs. Warner wouldn't mind if they took the cookies with them. But Mr. Warner would tell everyone that they had stolen food from him before running away.

In the wigwam, everything is shared. At camp, everything

148

belongs to everyone. But this is not a wigwam, Echohawk thought.

"Your cookies are very good," he said.

"Thank you, Jonathan. Have some more."

"I say . . . your cookies are good," Bamaineo said.

Mrs. Warner laughed. "You may have some more too, Bamaineo."

They each picked up a fistful of cookies.

"We'll leave a trail of cookies behind us when we start for Boston," said Joshua Warner. "He'll follow us gladly. All you have to do is feed him black-walnut cookies for the rest of his life."

"He can understand a lot of what you're saying," Jerusha Warner said angrily. "Do you want him to know what you have planned for him?"

"Nonsense! Jonathan, what did I just say?"

Echohawk froze. He glanced at Bamaineo, who had turned his face down toward his plate and was popping a cookie into his mouth. Bamaineo was gripping his tea mug hard.

Echohawk turned his face down toward his plate, too. "You said . . . the cookies are very good." He held on to his tea mug and waited.

"Do you see, Jerusha? He doesn't understand."

"I'm sure he did, Joshua. One of these mornings we're going to find the two of them gone."

Echohawk held his breath. *Do not let your face show anything, little brother. They are watching us.* Bamaineo calmly reached for another black-walnut cookie.

"More tea?" Mrs. Warner asked.

"Thank you," the brothers said together.

After evening corn, they did their homework just as on a normal school night, and they ate the rest of the cookies. They went upstairs when Mrs. Warner bade them good night. They sank into the corn-husk mattress for the last time.

"Look at my present, Echohawk." Moonlight flooded in through the cracks between the logs. Bamaineo held a piece of paper in front of his brother's face. Echohawk read in the silver moonlight:

> Jerusa Warnar,
> Thank you with helping our English.
> We like you.
> Now good bigh.
> Bamaineo

"You have to make your name here." Bamaineo pointed to the bottom of the paper. He gave his brother a piece of charcoal.

"When did you make this?"

"After noon corn. But I have been practicing."

Echohawk gave him a hard look. "Where? Where have you made these words before?"

Bamaineo pointed to his forehead and grinned. "I have been practicing here."

Echohawk wrote "Echohawk" at the bottom of the paper.

"No, you have to make 'Jonathan.'"

"That is not my name," Echohawk whispered angrily. "I told you not to call me that."

Bamaineo put his hand on his arm. "My brother, Mrs. Warner does not even know who Echohawk is. Please."

Echohawk sighed and drew an arrow next to his name. He wrote "Jonathan" next to it.

Bamaineo rolled the paper up again and hid it in his waist pouch. He lay down again.

"I hope our father is coming for us," he said in a worried voice. "I hope we do not have to leave the Muhekunetuk."

"We will have to leave anyway," Echohawk said sadly. "Even if Glickihigan does come home."

"Why?"

"Look at me, Bamaineo."

When Bamaineo turned over, Echohawk was sitting up and staring into space, his face glowing pale silver in the moonlight.

"Because our father can defeat a bear, but not a shaman from *Boston*. Go to sleep. We will start walking when the moon is down."

"I will stay awake with you."

But in a few moments Bamaineo was fast asleep.

CHAPTER FOURTEEN　　*The Creek and the Log*

THEY TRAVELED ALL NIGHT, walking in the water near the riverbank to leave no tracks. The snow was the same dull gray as the barrel of Thunderpath, the trees as black as the sky above them. Their moccasins and winter leggings were soaked with icy water. Echohawk would have liked nothing better than to stop and dry them over a fire. But he knew they would be just as wet again in ten steps or less.

Occasionally they heard great booming sounds, as heavy sheets of ice in the middle of the Muhekunetuk broke in two and were carried along in the swift current.

All night he had scanned the riverbank for trouble, for Glickihigan. Now it was almost dawntime, when the big animals came down to the river to drink. Echohawk tried to forget his exhaustion; he would have to be extra alert.

Bamaineo stumbled next to him, trying to walk with his eyes closed. *We will have to stop soon,* Echohawk thought. *Rest, let him sleep awhile, and dry our feet.*

Echohawk's keen eyes caught the edge of something:

152

a dark shape darted behind a hemlock tree in front of them. He yanked Bamaineo behind a nearby maple and stood directly behind him.

They stood as still as tree trunks, listening for any sound, watching for any movement.

Bamaineo turned his head slowly. "Human?" he breathed into Echohawk's ear. They both opened their mouths and breathed deeply through their noses, trying to catch the scent and taste of smoke. Bamaineo turned his head again and nodded.

"If we know he is one, he knows we are two," Echohawk murmured into his brother's ear. "He will wait until we move."

There was no movement, no sound behind the other tree.

Bamaineo turned his head slowly again. "He smells like our father, doesn't he, Echohawk?"

Echohawk slowly pulled his tomahawk from his belt. He could feel his brother pulling his knife out of his belt.

"Glick—Glickihigan," he whispered. "Father? Is it you?"

"Father," Bamaineo called out. "It is us!"

Glickihigan stepped from behind the tree.

"Manitou," he said, "thank you for saving my children." They ran to him.

"*School* was terrible," Bamaineo shouted, his arms tight around Glickihigan's waist. "Mr. Warner wants to take Echohawk away."

"Is this true?" their father asked. Echohawk, his arms around his father's neck, nodded into his shoulder.

"We have to leave this place anyway," Glickihigan said. "We have to leave now."

"Why?" Bamaineo asked. They both stepped back. "Why is your face painted black?"

Glickihigan's face was covered in a thick layer of charcoal. The black dust had settled into deep lines of sadness around his eyes and mouth.

"Everyone in camp is dead," he said softly. "A white man's sickness came. I do not know which one. Everyone is gone. Maybe ten suns ago."

"Gahko? Makwa?" Echohawk stammered. "Dead?"

"Tanebao Sachem?" Bamaineo asked. "Wapakwe?"

"Do not say their names," Glickihigan said quickly.

"Ten suns ago—that means the starfires are out. Are we dead too?" Bamaineo asked. In the half-light of dawn, Echohawk could see his brother pinching himself.

"That is just a story, Bamaineo," Glickihigan said in a faraway voice. "To frighten children, especially girls, so they will grow up learning to watch a starfire closely."

"Where are we going, Father?" Echohawk asked.

"We will head west to the Ohio River. We will live out our days among our brothers the Delaware.

"We must ask Manitou to leave the sickness here. Maybe we can run faster than the evil spirits who carry it with them. We must move quickly. We will go back the way you came."

"But Father," Bamaineo protested, "Echohawk saw my spirit-brother at the Freezing Moon. He told him to wait for me at camp. He is in camp waiting for me."

Glickihigan smiled fondly at his younger son. "Your spirit-brother always knows where you are, Bamaineo. He will find you."

"That leaves Schodac, the camp of your boyhood," Echohawk said. "The last of the Mohican camps on the Muhekunetuk."

"They have already left. I saw them in the Ohio country. All the Delaware are going west; they are all leaving their countries. I wanted to persuade Tanebao Sa —I wanted to see if our camp could go west, too. I was too late in returning.

"Bamaineo, while your brother is hunting, I will tell you everything I know about the People on our way to the Ohio country. You must remember everything."

Glickihigan rubbed his face hard. He rubbed the charcoal from one hand onto Echohawk's face, the charcoal from the other hand onto Bamaineo's face.

"We will go now."

They changed into fresh leggings and moccasins in the dawntime. Bamaineo wiggled his toes in the soft, warm moccasins and looked wistfully at Echohawk.

"We have been walking in the Muhekunetuk, so Mr. Warner would not see our tracks in the snow," Echohawk said.

"Good thinking," Glickihigan nodded. "But now there are three sets of tracks, and we are traveling toward Mr. Warner."

"Does that mean we no longer have to walk in the

river?" Bamaineo asked. "My feet are only now warm."

Glickihigan smiled fondly at his younger son. "Your feet will stay warm, Bamaineo."

At the island before *Saratoga-on-the-Hudson*, they trudged all the way up to the clearing above the river to avoid the town. It was odd, looking down on the school-house, cabin, and barn from such a distance. Echohawk sensed an uneasiness and saw the frantic movements of people in the school yard.

They know we are gone.

"Echohawk," Bamaineo whispered. With a stricken look on his face he pulled the roll of paper out of his waist pouch. "I forgot her present."

"Little brother," Echohawk sighed. "We cannot go back. It is too late."

They both saw Mrs. Warner shoot out of the cabin and run toward the school. She was wringing her hands. Her sobs rang out in the still morning air.

Bamaineo unrolled the paper and poked it between two tree branches. "Perhaps she will find her present here, Echohawk."

"Perhaps."

They walked the rest of the day without speaking, without stopping for morning corn or noon corn. The sun was bright red and dropping out of the gray winter sky when Glickihigan finally spoke.

"How much English did you learn in that school?" he asked Echohawk in English.

Echohawk smiled a little and answered his father in

English. "We learned a lot. We . . . studied every day. We . . . practiced hard. We . . . spoke English with our friends."

"That is good."

"Father, how many . . . white men live . . . in the Ohio country?"

"None. But they will be there soon."

Glickihigan stopped, turned around, and switched to Mohican. "Bamaineo is falling farther and farther behind. When did you start walking?"

Echohawk looked behind him too. Bamaineo stumbled and fell into the snow. He stood up slowly and wiped his eyes with his deerskin sleeves.

"Last night, when the moon went down," he answered in Mohican.

Glickihigan shook his head. "We will have to stop at sunset then. Bamaineo is only eight winters. He is too exhausted to walk much farther.

"I have been thinking. . . . You were right to leave *Saratoga-on-the-Hudson*, my son. But you did not run like a rabbit. There is a difference. I have thought about the shaman's claim since the dawntime." His father looked ashamed. "I cannot think of a way I could have helped you. We have no rights in our own land."

"I had the same thought."

"Yes, I know. . . . Bamaineo," Glickihigan called out. "Come here. Why are you crying? Do you see our brother the sun? He has been traveling for a long time, just like you. When he sleeps, you will sleep."

They waited for Bamaineo to catch up with them.

"Give me your pack," Glickihigan said.

"I can carry it!" Bamaineo sobbed.

"Yes, you can. I am very proud of you. You have carried this pack all night and for one sun. But now it is my turn."

They walked until sundown, then made an overnight camp with no fire. Glickihigan reached into his waist pouch and brought out nokekik for evening corn. He mixed the parched corn with clean snow while Bamaineo wrapped his bearskin blanket around him.

"He is too tired to eat," Echohawk said. He lifted the top of the bearskin and looked inside. "He is asleep already."

"He will not be too tired to eat tomorrow. Echohawk, your brother is healthy and he has grown. You have taken good care of him for me."

"It was hard. It is hard to look after a young one, to keep him in my mind all the time."

Glickihigan smiled. "It is hard work, work that never stops."

"Father, when will we get to Iroquois country?"

"In three moons. They live over the *Catskills* and by the narrow lakes."

"How will we get there?"

"We will walk toward *Albany*, then turn west and over the *Catskills*. We will have to be very careful around the narrow lakes. The Iroquois have their winter camps there. I am hoping they will be gone by the time we arrive. Only then will we follow the Susquehanna south, and turn west when she divides. Her western half will show us the way to the Three Sisters—the Allegheny and the Monongahela River join to make the Ohio. If we push hard, we will reach the Ohio River by the Fish Running Moon, but with Bamaineo with us—"

"Glickihigan, how did you cross Iroquois country and back again without being caught?"

"Echohawk, tell me the rules of hunting."

He hesitated. Knowing the rules of hunting had once been as automatic as breathing. The rules weren't something he knew, they were something he *was*. But how many suns had passed since he had walked downriver to the English camp? It seemed like a lifetime ago.

"Have I forgotten?" he asked, panic edging into his voice. "And what do the Iroquois have to do with hunting?"

"Tell me. Quickly—without thinking."

"No talking at any time. Look for tracks along the river. Then walk silently into the wind and have no human smell. Stay off the horizons so the animals will not see me against the sky. Look for tiny movements and listen for quick noises, look for horizontal shapes against the vertical trees. If I do make a noise, freeze, because animals cannot see stillness, only movement. The best places for hunting are where two places meet—forest and clearing, swamp and dry land, creek and log. The best times for hunting are dawntime and evening when animals are eating and drinking. Sight, hearing, smell, touch, taste: These are hunting tools Manitou has given us so we will not be hungry."

"You have not forgotten anything," Glickihigan said proudly. "When you are the hunted, the same rules apply."

"Why . . . did you say a white man's sickness?"

"Our brothers of the Canadas, the Micmacs, call whites 'the poison people' because they brought so much sickness with them when they crossed the Sun's Salt Sea. Sickness we have never seen before. Our medicine is not strong enough."

"I am very sorry," Echohawk said in a small voice.

"Yes, I am very sorry, too."

"That is not what I meant. I am sorry for the sickness. It is our fault. If whites had never crossed the Sun's Salt Sea—"

"Do you think I blame *you*?" Glickihigan asked in astonishment. "No, Echohawk, no. When I was in camp, looking into the faces of our dead, *our* dead, all I could think about was your face and your brother's face among them. No," he said firmly. "I have two sons. I do not blame you."

Echohawk sighed in relief. "You always know what I am thinking. Do you know what I am thinking now? Something good."

Glickihigan smiled at him. "You are thinking that there were many things you liked about the white man's camp."

"*Cookies* especially. They are little sweet cakes with

black walnuts inside them. I was eating these *cookies* at sundown last night. And drinking hot tea."

He took a bite of his evening corn nokekik. It tasted like burned corn and the leather of his father's waist pouch.

"*Cookies* have a good flavor, Father."

"Ah. So you did like something from *Saratoga-on-the-Hudson.*"

"Yes. I liked many things and some of the people. But I would never have gone with them. To *Boston* I mean."

"I had the same thought. Go to sleep, my son. You must be very tired. I will wake you when the moon goes down. You can stand your watch then. It is so good to see you both."

"It is good to see you, too. Good night, Father."

In the morning, Echohawk and Glickihigan divided most of the contents of Bamainco's pack between them.

"You are no longer tired, Bamainco?" Glickihigan asked.

"No."

"Good. Then we can begin."

Echohawk walked in front all day, watching for game, for trouble. Glickihigan never stopped talking; his voice sounded like the drone of bees: "Never forget that the Creator, Kishelemukong, caused the Great Turtle to rise from the sea, so the plants, the animals, and the People could live on his back. As long as we are here, Great Turtle Island will stay on his shell. If we go, then everything will disappear with us.

"Never forget the names of our ancient villages. Kaunaumeek was the place of our great council fire. This place is now called *Stockbridge,* Massachusetts, by the English. To the west were Scaticook, Monemius, and Potic. I grew up in Schodac. Schodac is near *Albany.* It was in Schodac that Henry Hudson first came ashore and met your great-great-great-grandfathers. Who would have thought . . ."

They stopped at sundown. The Sugar Maple Moon rose and lit up the snow, the ice, and the river. This time Echohawk mixed the nokekik with clean snow. Bamaineo burrowed into his bearskin as though it were a cave and fell asleep instantly.

"Our nokekik is almost gone," Echohawk said. "Tomorrow I will hunt for us."

The next morning they ate the rest of the nokekik for morning corn. As Echohawk was leaving to hunt, Bamaineo stared miserably into a small fire while his father told him about paints.

"Never forget our paints, what they mean, what they stand for: black for grief, purple for royalty. Your mother was our sachem's sister. This is why we always wore purple paint at our ceremonies, did you know that? I had to fight hard for Echohawk's right to wear the purple, too. Blue and yellow are for Sun Festivals, green for hunting and the Moon of Ripe Berries, red for war.

"I will tell you how to make these paints, so you can make them yourself someday. Always use walnut oil to

162

mix the paints. Green comes from oak leaves, yellow from ash bark; white maple bark mixed with charcoal makes blue. The purple comes from the tiny purple flowers that grow in the Strawberry Moon, black from— "

Poor Bamaineo, Echohawk thought. *He will not remember.*

Echohawk found deer tracks along the riverbank. White air bubbles flowed under the thin, translucent spring ice. With the butt of Thunderpath he broke a hole in the ice. He stripped off his clothes and soaked in the icy water as long as he could stand it, the current tugging at his long hair.

Since he'd been wearing the same clothes all winter, he decided to hunt in just his moccasins and breechcloth. The last thing he wanted was a human smell to scare the deer away.

Skin that smells like clean water . . .

Echohawk shook his head hard. "No memories today," he said firmly. He wrung as much water as he could out of his hair to keep it from freezing. Already he heard an odd tinkling sound around his ears: frozen hair.

He followed deer tracks up the steep west bank of the Muhekunetuk to a clearing. Three deer stood nosing and pawing the snow, looking for new grass. Echohawk lay flat in the snow and clenched his teeth to keep them from chattering. He fired. As one deer fell, the others scattered.

He left a gift, a small pile of his father's tobacco, near where the deer fell.

"Thank you, sister," Echohawk said. "Thank you for giving your life so my family can live." He slung the deer over his shoulders and went back to the riverbank for his clothes.

Back at the camp Glickihigan quickly skinned the deer and laid the steaming meat in the snow.

"We can have no fires in Iroquois country," he said. "While this meat cooks, wrap this fresh deerskin around you, take Thunderpath, and hunt again. Bamaineo will wash out your clothes. We will carry the venison with us and meet you downriver."

Glickihigan and Bamaineo stayed on the river's edge, Glickihigan talking an endless stream of words. Echohawk hunted far up the riverbank and came back to them again just before dusk, another deer draped over his shoulders.

"We will cook this deer tonight, Echohawk," his father said. "It is only a short distance now. We must hurry before darkness comes."

"*What* is a short distance?"

"We are almost there," Glickihigan said, half to himself.

The light was fading when Glickihigan stopped abruptly. He studied the trees, the stones along the riverbank, the earth itself. He stood lost in thought. Bamaineo lay down on the cold riverbank and closed his eyes.

"Echohawk," Glickihigan said softly, "do you see those twin tamaracks standing so tall? Over there."

"Yes, I see them."

"You will walk to them, turn right, then walk straight ahead another three hundred steps."

"Up the riverbank? Why?"

"We will never see the Muhckunetuk again, and time travels in a circle. Your thirteenth winter, and your childhood, ended yesterday at the Sugar Maple Moon. You are a man today. Go; we will be here when you return."

Glickihigan turned to Bamaineo.

"Bamaineo, while we are gathering firewood I will tell you about our feathers and what they mean. The eagle for purity, the wild turkey for cleverness, the hawk is the hunter. Wake up."

Echohawk walked toward the twin tamaracks, keeping a sharp eye out for more deer tracks.

When you are the hunted, the same rules apply.

We will travel in the evening and night and sleep under fresh pine branches by day. It does not matter if we leave tracks in the snow—the freezing and thawing will make the tracks look old. Iroquois always smell like tobacco; I will ask Glickihigan to stop smoking so we can smell them but they cannot smell us. We will bathe in the river water every day, or at least bathe with snow. We should soak all our clothes, too.

But if we are ghosts, what difference will it make? If we are already dead, because our starfires are out, the Iroquois cannot kill us again.

A white man walked right past him heading north. Darkness clung to the man like a bearskin. He didn't even nod his head or look in Echohawk's direction. A ghost?

We are the ghosts. Glickihigan is wrong; the starfire burning is not just a story. That man did not even see me.

He turned at the tamaracks, then climbed uphill in a straight line. Soon after, Echohawk stopped to rest on a hollow log near a creekbed and tried not to think about his feet, numb with cold. *Two deer today,* he thought proudly. *I have not forgotten anything. We can start walking again after I see whatever it is our father wants me to see.*

Echohawk saw little tracks like human hands in the thawing creek mud and smiled. *Raccoons,* he thought automatically. *A raccoon family lives in this log. How do I know that?*

He thought about raccoons on this same patch of creekbed, holding and eating their fish as if it were corn on the cob. But that was a hot summer day, and a long time ago.

I have sat on this log before. There were ants crawling across my legs in single file. But how can that be? I have never been this far south before.

Other thought pictures crowded into his mind, like the deer rushing and pushing each other toward the hunt fence. Ants in single file, a hand trap for fish, a raccoon family eating purple huckleberries. Kittens as silent as stones. Footsteps and fire arrows, smoke, hiding in this log, sheets of flame, screaming, corn pudding spreading out like a fan, the sweet smell of the horses, a man whose skin smells like clean water—

Glickihigan!

Echohawk ran. Heart pounding, muscles crawling, panting, rushing across the creekbed and scrambling over an overgrown path—

Glickihigan!

The blackened wood of the collapsed cabins, now covered with mold, mud, and leaves. Inside the first cabin, dirt floor, roof gone, tables, chairs, barrels all black and burned, broken blue dishes all the way from South Carolina.

There! The corner I had to stand in when I spent too much time in the woods! He thought he saw his four-year-old self whimpering in the corner in the slanting morning sunshine.

There! There! Our table! He thought he saw his four-year-old self eating a bowl of corn pudding for lunch. When his mother's back is turned, Jonathan will sneak outside to his favorite hollow log.

Jonathan, have you been playing in the woods again? Come sit by the fire, you must be cold.

Ghosts, spirits, I am dead too, a burial ground—

Jonathan Starr, I mean now! The Indians will get you.

Don't scare him, Celia.

My last words in English to you are these. We are Mohicans.

Glickihigan!

"Never forget our totems, Bamaineo, our clans," Glickihigan was saying. The venison was smoking and sputtering over the fire. "In your time there were the

Turtle, the Wolf, and the Bear. But once there were fifty clans: the Moose, the Elk, the Deer, the Eagle, the Hawk, the Wild Turkey, the Yellow Eel, and many more. Each totem had ten wigwams; once your mother's camp reached all the way to our waterfall. This is not the first time a white man's sickness has come."

"No more," Bamaineo cried. "How can I remember everything?"

"What you do not remember I will tell you again, so you can tell your son. Never forget our mnoti, the bag of peace. With mnoti we can make treaties with all tribes, all nations, including English, French, Dutch. Surely we can all live on Great Turtle Island together. The sacred objects inside the bag, the beaver pelts and silver ropes, were brought to us from the sky—"

Echohawk screamed like a hawk after prey.

Bamaineo shouted, "Echohawk is back!"

"You were there! You killed them!" he shouted in English to his father. "You killed my mother, my sisters, my brother. You killed my father! My name is Jonathan Starr and *you killed them!*"

Glickihigan looked calmly at his son, who panted and shivered in a bloody deerskin, his hair tangled and caught in brambles, his eyes as wild as those of a hunted animal.

He spoke to him in Mohican. "Last night," he said softly, "I saw your mother on the east side of the Muhekunetuk. She was waving good-bye. She told me what a mistake it has been, not to tell you.

"As the Starr man died, he shouted 'Jonathan, Jonathan.' After I found you hiding in the log, I realized that was you."

"Who killed the Starrs?"

"All of us: Makwa, Nehjao, Tamaqua—you do not remember him. He was killed soon after. It was such a long time ago," Glickihigan said in a pleading voice. "And they are all dead together now."

"How could you not tell me this?"

"I wanted to, so many times I have wanted to. Almost nine winters now. But the more I grew to love you, the less courage I had to tell you. They are all dead together now," he said again.

Echohawk was crying so hard, Glickihigan and Bamaineo were deerskin blurs in front of his eyes. He fell to his knees. Thunderpath shook in his hands. Bamaineo gently took the barrel with both hands and lowered it softly to the forest floor.

As Echohawk lay weeping in the snow, the whole forest seemed to echo his cries, as though it were filled with sobbing and wailing ghosts.

The few bones they could find they buried the Mohican way: the bones standing upright and the things the Starrs would need in the next world—spoons, forks, cups, and dishes—placed around them. The grave was covered with wood, mud was packed on top. Birch bark was then lashed on with long branches of hickory. To Echohawk, the grave looked like a little wigwam, the family gathered around a starfire.

Echohawk placed one last handful of pine needles at the very top. He stood back and the other two waited.

"Welcome them, Manitou," he said softly. "Welcome them into the circle of time. To wherever they are going, to whatever they hope for, please welcome them."

He turned to his father and his brother. "We can go now. To the Ohio country. I do not blame you."

Glickihigan replied, "It is good country."

AFTERWORD

About the Lenapes or the Delawares

In their own language, Lenape means "the People." The Lenapes were the first Native Americans the Dutch and English met when they came to North America.

There were once at least twenty nations among the Lenapes. Among them were the Wappingers, Esopus, Munsees, Mohicans, Unamis, Raritans, Massapequas, Wampanoags, Nipmucs, Canarsees, Manhattans, Montauks, Susquehannans, Catskills, Hackensacks, Rockaways, Nanticokes, Minisinks, Unahachaugs, and Powhatans. (Pocahontas was a Powhatan Lenape.)

Many more tribes, including the Illinois, the Shawnees, and the Anasazis of the southwest, can claim kinship to the ancient Lenape.

The Lenapehoking, or the Land of the Lenapes, once spanned what is now eastern New York State including New York City and Long Island, eastern Pennsylvania, New Jersey, Delaware, Maryland, and Virginia.

The Lenapes had been living in the Lenapehoking since the days of the mastodons, but by the 1740s most had died of disease or warfare or had been pushed west into what is now western Pennsylvania and eastern Ohio.

Glickihigan's Three Sisters—where the Monongahela and Allegheny Rivers join to form the Ohio River—is now Pittsburgh, Pennsylvania.

The Lenapes believed that everything, from the mightiest bear to the smallest ant, had a *manetuwak,* or a spirit. Water, stones, wood, even a snowflake, had a *manetuwak.* The Creator, Kishelemukong, made the world, then stepped back to make room for all the other *manetuwak.* Although Kishelemukong gave the Lenapes the Lenapehoking, they believed he wasn't involved in their everyday lives. The Lenape prayed to Manitou, their own Great Spirit, and at the same time knew Kishelemukong was listening.

Why are the Lenapes called the Delawares?

In 1610 the first governor of Jamestown, Virginia, was a man named Baron Thomas West de la Warr. The Delaware River was named after him. The people living on the riverbank and in nearby villages became known as "de la Warr's Indians," and the name stuck. The Lenapes have been calling themselves after Baron Thomas West de la Warr for more than three hundred years.

Today there are very few Delawares left. Most live in Oklahoma and in Ontario, Canada. Another group, the Stockbridge-Munsee band of Mohicans, have lived in Wisconsin since the 1820s. Almost two hundred years ago James Fenimore Cooper wrote a book called *The Last of the Mohicans,* but he was mistaken in thinking they were gone. *Echohawk* could not have been written

172

without the Mohicans' help, and I dedicate this book to their courage and perseverance.

About the Haudenosaunee or the Iroquois
In the Onondaga language, Haudenosaunee means "the People of the Longhouse." (A longhouse is a traditional Iroquois bark-and-sapling house shaped like a loaf of brown bread.) The Mohawks, Oneidas, Onondagas, Cayugas, Senecas, and later the Tuscaroras have called themselves Haudenosaunee for almost six hundred years. They live in New York State and Ontario. In colonial days their Native American neighbors believed the Iroquois to be a fierce and warlike people. The word "Iroquois" comes from the Algonquin and means "terrifying man." Again, the name stuck, probably because European explorers met the Algonquins first and were warned by them about the Iroquois.

About the Algonquins
The native people of North America are generally divided into ten language groups. The Algonquins live across Canada, in the Rocky Mountains, and along the eastern seaboard of the United States. "Algonquin" is their word for "language." The Delawares belong to the Algonquin group of Native Americans: Smaller Algonquin nations united to form the larger nation of the Delawares.

Great Turtle Island
How could a Delaware in the Eastern woodlands know

about the glaciers in Alaska and Canada and the prairies and deserts in the American West? They knew what North America looked like because of ancient trading routes among the nations. They also knew about these places from *The Wallam Olum,* a collection of Lenape stories collected as pictographs and now published as a book (Avery Press, 1993). According to the Delawares' oral tradition, the ancient Lenapes left central China thousands of years ago and gradually migrated to the eastern seaboard of North America.

The characters

Glickihigan and Bamaineo were real people. They were Turtle clan Mohicans who left the Hudson River Valley in the 1740s and were living in the missionary town of Gnadenhutten, Ohio, by the 1770s. In March 1782 American troops led by Lieutenant Colonel David Williamson killed ninety Mohican and other Delaware residents in Gnadenhutten. One of those killed was an old man named Isaac Glickihigan. He was described as "a sachem, and was noted among his countrymen, for superior wisdom and courage." There is no record, at least none I could find, of what happened to Bamaineo.

Jonathan Starr is pure fiction, but Starr is a family name of mine. The Starrs lived in colonial New York and Connecticut. The Lenapes or Delawares have always been a source of fascination for me, because one of the New York Starrs was born a Delaware woman.

About the Hudson River Valley

I used the Village of Saratoga as a model for my river town of Saratoga-on-the-Hudson. The Village of Saratoga was founded in 1690. The local patroon family, the original Dutch settlers on this part of the Hudson, were the Schuylers. On November 28, 1745, the Village of Saratoga was burned to the ground by French and Huron marauders. Thirty people were killed, thirty buildings were burned, including the Schuyler home, and one hundred captives were taken to New France (Quebec).

In the early part of this century the Village of Saratoga, New York, was renamed Schuylerville. The Schuyler home has been rebuilt and still stands just south of the town.

In colonial days, the Hudson River Valley was an interesting mix of people. The Algonquins, the Iroquois, the Dutch, and the English all called it home. French and aboriginal Canadians traveled south to Albany to trade their furs. The English hired Irishmen and Hessian Germans as soldiers for their Hudson River armies. There were slaves from Africa living in the towns and fortresses. In many ways, the Hudson River Valley in those days was like our country today, a mix of many different kinds of people.

GLOSSARY

Abenaki (ah beh NAH kee): an Algonquin tribe in Maine

bamain (bam MANE): a male elk

Bamaineo (bam MANE ee oh): Bounding Elk

Gahko (GAH KOH): Crane Dance

Gishikshawkipet (gih shik SHAW kih pet): The Sun's Salt Sea (the Atlantic Ocean)

Glickihigan (glick ih HIG an): Gunsight

Gnadenhutten (ja NAY den hut ten): Little Huts of Grace; a missionary town in Ohio

Hepte (HEP teh): Swan

Kaunaumeek (KAW naw meek): an ancient village

Kipemapekun (kih pee MAP ee kan): the Great Lakes

Kishelemukong (kih shel MOO kong): the Creator

Lenape (leh NAH peh): the People

Loxpa (LOX PAH): Panther Trail

Makwa (MAHK WAH): Bear

Makwasi (mahk WAH see): Bear Woman

manetuwak (mah nih TOH wahk): spirit

Manitou (mah nih TOH): the Great Spirit

Micmac (MIK MAHK): an Algonquin tribe in northern New Brunswick, in the Canadas

mnoti (NOH tee): peace; a bag symbolizing peace

Mohawk (MOH hawk): a tribe of the Iroquois

Mohican (moh HIH can): the Wolf People

Monemius (moh NEE mee us): an ancient village

Muhekunetuk (muh hee KUN nee took): The Water
Is Never Still (the Hudson River)

naahmao (nah may OH): a wild turkey

Nehjao (neh JAY oh): Big Wolf

nokekik (NOKE KICK): parched corn

Potic (POH tick): an ancient village

sachem (SAH chem): an Algonquin leader or king

Scaticook (SCAH tih cook): an ancient village

Schodac (SHOH dahk): an old Mohican village

Sokoki (shoh KOH kee): an Algonquin tribe in Vermont

Tamaqua (TAH mah quah): Beaver

Tanebao (tan eh BAY oh): Great Turtle

Tooksetuk (TOOK seh TOOK): Little Wolf

Walamocawapallanewa (WOO lah mah cah wah pah
LAH neh wah): He Speaks Truly of the White Hawk

Wapakwe (wah PAHK weh): Opossum

Windigo (win DIH goh): an evil spirit

SOURCES

Arden, Harvey. "The Iroquois: Keepers of the Fire." *National Geographic* (September 1987).

Ballantine, Betty and Ian, eds. *The Native Americans.* Washington, D.C.: Smithsonian Books, 1994.

Billard, Jules, ed. *The World of the American Indian.* Washington, D.C.: National Geographic Society, 1974.

Demos, John. *The Unredeemed Captive.* New York: Alfred A. Knopf, 1994.

Dovell, S. D. W. *Handbook of American Indian Languages.* Lincoln, NE: University of Nebraska Press, 1966.

Galloway, Colin G. *The Abenaki.* New York: Chelsea House Publishers, 1988.

Gnadenhutten Historical Society. *Massacre at Gnadenhutten.* Gnadenhutten, OH: Gnadenhutten Historical Society, 1803. Reprint June 1988.

Grolier, Claudia. *Algonquian Hunters of the Eastern Woodlands.* Toronto: Grolier Ltd., 1983.

Grumet, Robert S. *The Lenapes.* New York: Chelsea House Publishers, 1953.

Hyde, George. *Indians of the Woodlands from Prehistoric Times to 1725.* Norman, OK: University of Oklahoma Press, 1962.

McCutchen, David, trans. *The Wallam Olum, The Red Record.* Atlanta: Avery Press, 1993.

Miller-Heath, Leah, Tribal Planner and Wisdomkeeper, The Stockbridge-Munsee Band of Mohicans, Route 1, Bowler, Wisconsin.

Richter, Conrad. *The Light in the Forest.* New York: Dodd, Mead & Company, 1953. Reprint Amereon, Ltd.

Roseboom, Eugene, and Francis Weisenburger. *A History of Ohio.* Edited by James Rodabaugh. Columbus, OH: Ohio Historical Society Press, 1964. Rev. ed. 1972.

Schuylerville Historical Society, Schuylerville, New York.

Siegal, Beatrice. *Indians of the Northeast Woodlands Before and After the Pilgrims.* New York: Walker & Co., 1992.

Smithsonian Bureau of Ethnology. *Guide to North American Indian Tribes.* Washington, D.C.: Smithsonian Press, 1979.

Western Reserve Historical Society, Hudson, Ohio.

ABOUT THE AUTHOR

Lynda Durrant has always been fascinated by the part of the story that James Fenimore Cooper didn't tell in *The Last of the Mohicans* and wanted to tell it herself, but she didn't want simply to write a prequel. "It bothered me that, because of James Fenimore Cooper, many people think there are no more Mohicans," she says. Motivated also by the Delaware heritage in her own family, Ms. Durrant decided to write about the Hudson River Valley as it truly was. *Echohawk,* her first book, shows how the Mohicans' ancient ways mixed with the adopted ways of the English colonists.

Ms. Durrant has a double master's degree in writing and teaching English from the University of Washington in Seattle, and teaches remedial reading to children. She lives with her husband and son on a horse farm in rural Ohio.